CROSSFIRE AT DAINGERFIELD

JACK R, STANLEY

*To Larry,
Enjoy!
Jack R. Stanley*

Wrightbridge Press

To Mary Lee
with whom all things are possible.

Crossfire At Daingerfield

Copyright © 2022 by Jack R. Stanley.
All rights reserved.
ISBN: 978-1-954212-47-3

This book may not be copied or reproduced, in whole or in part, by any means, electronic, mechanical or otherwise, without written permission from the publisher except by a reviewer who may quote brief passages in his/her review.
This is a work of fiction. Any resemblance to any persons, events or localities is purely coincidental and beyond the intent of the author and publisher.

Credits:
Cover
Kevin Diamond

Edited by
Mary Lee Stanley
and
Rose Marie Reed

Wrightbridge Press
jacks@wrightbridgepress.com
www.thefictionwritersnotebook.com
www.jackrstanley.com

TWO FREE E-BOOKS

[Murder in Muleshoe]
If you were murdered would they try to find the killer or plan him a parade?

[Guns Along The Rio]
In 1858, two fresh-off-the-ranch 17-year-olds join the Texas Rangers. What could possibly go wrong?

GO TO: http://eepurl.com/dKEi_Y

CHAPTER 1

Mathias Gaynes hurriedly tried to saddle a painted pony in the dark barn. When the small barn door creaked open, and lantern light spilled in, he went for his '73 Colt Single Action Army Revolver. But he heard the cocking of two others and froze.

Two men entered. The tallest of the pair was Herculean, at almost seven feet tall with a babyface. Leading the way, however, was a shorter man, almost 30. He held his .44 Smith and Wesson in a rock-solid grip.

"Easy, Wilkes," the horse thief stammered. "I didn't mean for nothin' t' happen t' Edmonia. It was an accident."

"Rape isn't an accident."

"Well, it didn't mean nothing. I was jest havin' a little fun."

"You think she saw it that way?"

"No, no," the thief stammered, trying to think of something — anything — to get him out of this.

The man called Wilkes was rangy, with tight muscles and no slack in him. He was less than 6 feet, but a commanding presence dominated the space. He stepped over until the barrel of his pistol was right against Mathias's chest. The bigger man by the door had a Winchester in his hands. The rifle was dwarfed like a toy.

"I know I done wrong — and — and I'm sorry. Really, really sorry. I got carried away."

"It's way past bein' sorry, Mathias. You could have stopped — at any time. But you didn't."

"What are you going to do to me?"

"Drop your gun belt — and then your pants. Next, open the back flap on your union suit."

"What?"

"We're going to lean you over the stall — and Big John is going to have — a little fun — with you."

The rapist glanced at that towering man a few steps back. Mathias Gaynes swallowed. He shivered at the idea of what Big John could do to him. He tried to step back, but there was nowhere for him to go.

"I'm not going to tell you again," Wilkes said. "Do it or die right where you're standing."

"No. No!" Mathias begged. "Not that. No man's ever going to do that to me — especially not Big John."

The barn door opened again, and a farmer in overalls stepped in carrying a shotgun.

"What's going on here?"

"Help me, mister," Mathias pleaded. "They're goin' t' kill me."

"After Big John gets through with you, we will," Wilkes said.

"What did he do?" the rancher asked.

"He was trying to steal your paint there. You can see the dun he's almost killed getting here."

"Raleigh's my best horse," the farmer said.

"Another minute and he'd be gone," Wilkes said.

"This is the boot heel of Missouri. We hang horse thieves in these parts," the farmer said, lowering his weapon. "Name's Ossie Duell. I'll get a rope."

"Not until after we're through with him," Wilkes said evenly, pressing his pistol into Mathias's breast bone.

"He also raped our younger sister," the large man said, slightly above a whisper.

"Nobody's goin' t' do that t' me!" Mathias tried to sound as if he had some say about it.

"Then go for your gun," Wilkes, and I'll kill you here."

Mathias's lips were dry. He tried to think back on the young woman he'd stripped and had under him only hours before. But it brought him no joy now.

The rapist grabbed at his Colt as Wilkes pulled the trigger and ripped apart Mathias's heart before the bullet shattered his spine and he sank to the dirt floor of the barn.

There was finally silence in the structure when Wilkes holstered his gun.

"Wilkes, I — I couldn't have done what you said," the big man said. "I could have killed him for what he did to Edmonia — but I couldn't have done that — other thing — not to anyone."

"I know, Big John," Wilkes said, patting his younger brother on his huge arm. "I never expected you to. It was all a bluff. I wanted him to feel a little of what Edmonia must have felt."

"Oh," Big John said, nodding his head. To the farmer, Big John said, "Our sister was seeing to her favorite mare's first fold. Wasn't due until tomorrow. We tried to tell her that, but she insisted on spending the night with her horse."

"That piece of garbage," Wilkes glanced over at the body of Mathias, "had his own ideas of what to do."

"Your name's Wilkes?" the farmer asked. "That ain't a popular name — not since Lincoln."

"I was born and named before the war."

The farmer studied the body of Mathias Gaynes.

"We bury horse thieves — after we hang 'em." He paused and then said, "This trash — I don't want him planted on my land."

"I'll see to it. How would you feel about doing some horse-trading?"

"I don't do no horse-trading at night."

"Mind if we spend the night in your barn? We're like to rub down and feed our mounts."

"Help yourself," Ossie Duell said. "But I don't want that dead thing on my land."

"I'll take care of it," Wilkes said. "Which way does your land run?"

"Five miles in every direction."

"Got an old blanket I can wrap him in? Horses don't like the smell of blood."

"Ma'll find something." The farmer left for the house.

"What you going to do with him, Wilkes?" Big John asked.

"Find someplace a good 10 miles away and pitch him in a ditch."

"You're not goin' t' bury him?"

Wilkes stooped and pulled Mathias Gaynes away from the wall.

"Coyotes and buzzards gotta eat, too."

CHAPTER 2

All the hard-used horses had been rubbed down, fed, and rested by the next morning. Even the dun Mathias Gaynes had tried to ride into the ground was back to looking strong and eager. Wilkes full-blooded bay and the Morgan Big John had ridden stood tall in their stalls, ready for a new day.

Farmer Ossie Duell, raw-boned, close-cut gray hair, called Wilkes and Big John to the spacious and comfortable kitchen at first light for breakfast. Kate Duell, Ossie called her "Ma," was big-boned, wide hipped. She had weather-tanned skin and pulled-back blonde hair. The woman was cheerful and a marvelous cook. She served plates piled high with pancakes, eggs, bacon, and grits. The fresh milk was cold, and the coffee steaming.

After asking a blessing on the meal, Duell said, "I figured out who you boys are. From Kentucky, I'd guess from the miles you'd ridden." Putting his coffee down, he added, "Your brands are Caley. Like I said last night, you're in Missouri now, but I don't figure you want anybody t' know it."

"No, sir," Wilkes said. "And I wish you'd forget you ever heard me called Wilkes."

"Can't remember a thing," the farmer said. "But if we're goin' t' do some horse-trading, I'll need a name for bills of sale."

"Ethan Andrews," Wilkes said after a moment.

"Mr. Andrews. Pleased t' meet you and your brother — "

"If you could — Big John was never here."

"Ghost in the night," Duell said.

"You serve a handsome table," Wilkes said to Mrs. Duell."

"Fed and raised six strong sons around this here table. Each one is bigger and stronger than his brother. I've also fed an ark load of farmhands over the seasons. So don't be bashful. If there's something you want and you don't see it — speak up."

"Thank ya', ma'am," Big John said. "I reckon we'll get our fill right here."

Out in front of the barn, the farmer checked over the horses Ethan and his brother had as well as the dun the rapist had ridden. The Morgan had strong legs and an impressive head with a straight profile. She also had large, prominent eyes, well-defined withers, laid-back shoulders, and an upright, well-arched neck.

"I've got nothing like this," Duell said. "I love t' have her on the place. Never had any animal this strong."

"You've got that, Grulla. He has to be almost 14 hands tall. He's not Morgan, but Big John just needs a strong ride t' get him back home on."

"I could do that, but I've have t' throw in a bunch more. I ain't goin'a cheat like that."

"How about your Raleigh and a strong packhorse for me?"

"Where you goin', Wilkes?" Big John asked.

"Kansas, maybe Colorado — could even go to California."

The farmer finished his inspection of Wilkes and Big John's horses. He said, "What if I swap you Raleigh and my blood bay. She is strong. And I'd throw in a pack-saddle crosstree and a whole load of supplies — last you a good two months — with a tarp you could use for a tent. And I'll throw in a little money t' make it even."

"I think we can make a deal, Mr. Duell."

"I'll go make out the bills of sale and get Ma started on the supplies."

When Big John and Wilkes were alone, the big man said, "Why are you doing this?"

"I killed a man, Big John — murdered him."

"If you hadn't, I would have."

"I know — but that's a burden I didn't want you to carry."

"No court is going to find you guilty."

"Maybe. But I can't take that chance — and I won't expose Edmonia for what happened to her. So my going away is the only way to handle this."

"What do I tell Ma and Pa? They'll miss you somethin' crazy."

"They'll understand. Just tell folks I got an itch and headed West. The less said about Edmonia, the better. She's the one who will need all the love and care she can get." After a moment, he said, "Say I just had to see what was over the next hill — maybe I got gold fever. Leave it at that."

"Edmonia'll miss you most of all."

"She'll understand — someday."

"Will we ever hear from you?"

"If you do — it'll be from Ethan Andrews."

"Ethan Andrews," Big John said to make sure he remembered.

"You're going to have to do some growing up — inside — Big John. Pa will leave the place to you."

"I can't run no horse farm."

"You'll have t' learn. Edmonia will help."

"What about Mathias?"

"Few people knew him — most who did didn't like him. They won't care he's gone. If anyone — the sheriff, let's say — asks — you don't know. You woke up a few days after I left and he was gone, too."

Big John took Ethan Andrews in his arms and hugged him for a long time.

"You know I'll miss you, too."

"I know. And I'll miss you, brother. But I can't figure any other way. You?"

The huge man shook his head.

CHAPTER 3

Ethan Andrews didn't go the way he had said. Instead, he turned southwest into Arkansas. He followed the Black River to the White River crossing. This was at the foot of the Boston Mountains in the Ozarks in Arkansas. That is when he came upon a broken-down wagon on the side of the trail.

One of the rear wheels had two broken spokes, and the wagon tongue was wedged over a rock and under the wagon. Ethan didn't see anyone around. There was a fresh grave nearby, stones piled on top of the packed dirt. He rode up to the back of the wagon and saw a body wrapped in a blanket. That's when he heard a sound of a Winchester being cocked.

"That's my Ma. Don't touch her!"

Ethan couldn't place the voice but knew it came from somewhere in the rocks and trees nearby. He raised his hands.

"No offense intended." He sat there a moment waiting for a response, but when none came, he offered, "Can I give you a hand?"

"The last men who passed this way stole everything they could carry."

The voice was young. Ten-year-old, Ethan figured — maybe 12.

"That's not me. I'll leave my guns on my saddle." Slowly Ethan unbuckled his gunbelt and rehooked it around his saddle horn. "I'm getting down — slowly."

He did as he said, keeping his hands raised, and walked over to the grave. A second was started beside the first, but it was no more than a foot deep.

"You thirsty — hungry?" Ethan was still trying to locate the kid.

"Two days," came the voice again, and Ethan saw the rifle sag over the edge of a boulder. "They shot a hole in the water barrel as the left just because they could."

"I got three canteens. All of them are full. You can help yourself."

"If I had been here, I would have killed them — both." A skinny boy stepped out from behind the boulder holding the rifle. "Pa sent me to fish — fetch us some food before we tried to get the wheel off. He must have tried to do it himself — and it killed him. He was wounded in the war and still carried a bullet in his chest."

"Was it the robbers that shot your water barrel full of holes?"

"That was the sound that brought me back. By the time I got here, they had come and gone. They took the mules with them."

"Why not get some water and food off my horse. There's some ham and beans in the saddlebags. I'll finish with your mother's grave."

The kid broke down sobbing and curled up in a ball. Ethan helped him back to what was left of the campfire circle of stones. He laid the rifle beside the boy and got a canteen and saddlebags. The boy guzzled from the canteen until Ethan pulled it away.

"Take it easy. Your stomach's empty. Too much too fast'll make you sick. When the kid nodded his understanding, Ethan handed him back the canteen.

The ground was dry but not too hard. Still, it took him an hour to finish the grave. By the time he'd finished, the boy was asleep beside the fire he'd started as water boiled in the pan.

Ethan lifted the woman from the wagon by himself. She was starting to get a little ripe, and he didn't think it would have been a good thing for the youngster to deal with. He secured the blanket around the body and used his rope to lower it into the ground. He filled in the grave and stacked rocks on it like the kid had done on his fathers.

Using his hatchet and his Bowie knife, Ethan cut some wood and fashioned a cross for each grave. They were driven into the ground before he woke the boy.

The kid cried and knelt between the graves for over half an hour. Finally, Ethan returned to the wagon. With the family Bible he'd found thrown in the dirt, he cleaned it off. Back at the graves, he found the 23rd Psalm. Standing behind the boy, he read the passage aloud. Then Ethan turned to Isaiah 41.

"Do not fear, for I am with you; do not be afraid, for I am your God. I will strengthen you; I will surely help you; I will uphold you with My right hand of righteousness. So do not fear, for I am with you; do not be dismayed, for I am your God. I will strengthen you and help you."

With that, Ethan closed the book and started reciting the Lord's prayer. The boy joined in about halfway through. Then, Ethan walked back to the fire quietly.

Eventually, the smell of bacon, beans, corn fritters, and coffee drew the youngster back to the circle of stones. Ethan spooned up a plate which was accepted eagerly.

"You drink coffee, yet?"

"Started last year."

Ethan poured him a cup.

When he was done, the boy said, "I don't know how to thank you for everything."

"No need," Ethan said. "I'm sorry those other sons of bitches didn't do the right thing." Then, after another moment, Ethan offered his hand. "I'm Ethan Andrews."

The youngster's grip wasn't strong, but a few fresh callouses were already building on his palm. "Bill. Bill Cooper."

"Pleasure, Bill. Where were you folks headed?"

"Texas, Pa said. That's before Mother came down with the fever."

"You farmers?"

"Wanted t' be. But Pa had a weak heart. Part of being wounded. He worked for a freight company after the war. Saved his money — he wanted to get us away from war — and the sea. We lived in what was left of Richmond." He thought a moment and then added, "Pa's brother owns his own ship. He's well off. He saw that we had a good wagon and everything we needed."

"Richmond? You've come a long way."

"I was afraid we'd never make it." He closed his eyes and tried to hold back tears. "What do I do now?"

"Seems t' me the first thing is to get your wagon fixed up. I suppose the robbers took your mules?"

The boy nodded. He was slight. His dark hair looked to have been cut around the edges of a bowl. Ethan figured he must have taken after his father.

Ethan sighed and said, "I figured as much. What's say we get that busted wheel off while there's still light. Tomorrow we'll make a travois t' haul it, and see where we can get it fixed."

"What's a — travois?"

"A couple of poles tied to the back of a horse. Indians use it instead of wagons. I never understood why. Now I can see the sense of it."

"I've got no money."

"I have a little. What's say we partner up and see what we can do?"

"Why would you do that?"

"Couldn't leave you here. I can't think of anything else t' do. Got any better ideas?" The boy shook his head, and Ethan asked, "You all right with that?"

"Mr. Andrews, I don't seem to have much of choice."

"Name's Ethan, Bill. Partners call each other by their first names."

CHAPTER 4

The bolt was still snug on the busted wheel. The wrench was in the dirt. Tryin' t' get it loose must have been what killed Bill Cooper's father, Ethan thought.

He wiped the dirt off the wrench fitted it to the bolt, so the handle hung off at about a 7 o'clock position. Then, using both hands, the muscles in the legs, his arms, and his back, Ethan twisted the bolt free of the slotted lock washer which held it in place on the center of the hub.

Next, they repositioned the wagon tongue only slightly from where Mr. Cooper had placed it before he died working on the wheel bolt. Bill and Ethan strained to lift the wagon, and then Ethan sat on the lever while Bill wrestled the wheel off the axle. Together they eased the wagon back on the very stone that had broken the two wheel spokes.

The effort had taken a toll on both man and boy. Bill's bellyache came back. Before they went to bed, he had groaned a little and clutched his middle.

They had bacon and dry biscuits for their evening meal.

"Hope it's not my cookin'," Ethan said. "I know I'm not very good — but I never made anybody sick before."

"It'll be OK," Bill said. "I think it's like my gulpin' the water when you first got here. "My stomach isn't used to food, I expect."

Even with Bill hurtin', they propped the wheel against the side of the wagon, unloaded the packhorse, unsaddled Ethan's paint, and placed bedrolls under the wagon for the night.

Although Ethan found sleep easily, he woke in the middle of the night to find Bill shaking and crying silently between his parent's graves.

By daybreak, Bill was back in his blanket and sleeping. Ethan stirred and built up the fire to start breakfast. He finished eating, and the boy continued to sleep, so Ethan turned to cleaning his weapons.

He carried two pistols, both Schofield model 3s with 5-inch barrels. One hung down from his gun belt on his right side, and the other fit in a horizontal holster on his left. He cleaned the pistols and both his and Bill's Winchesters. Ethan was sharpening his bowie knife when Bill sat up and looked around. It took a minute for him to catch up to where he was, who Ethan was, and what had happened.

Wiping his face, he said, "Why didn't you get me up — Ethan?"

"Thought you could use a little extra sleep after the last few days. Come get a cup of coffee. That'll start you off in fine shape."

The boy started to put on his boots when Ethan warned, "Not so quick. It's always a good idea to shake your boots out if you didn't sleep in them. Scorpians like the warmth you left behind and could give you a nasty surprise."

Bill understood and knocked his boots against a rock and shook them before pulling them on.

He ate a good breakfast and wiped out the pan before he and Ethan went looking for poles.

"Travois?" he asked once, noticing the hatchet had been sharpened.

"Right," Ethan said. "I'd say we'll looking for something about 2 inches across and a dozen feet long."

They found what they needed cut and stripped the branches before bringing the poles back to camp. Next, they set the cross-tree carrying saddle on the packhorse and bound the ends of polls together. Next, the used rope to secure the outer part of the wheel to each pole. Finally, they loaded the packhorse and secured the tarp over the load.

Bill tried to handle the saddling of the paint, but he was still a couple of inches too short for the job.

When everything was loaded and Ethan in the saddle, he extended a hand to Bill, who held back.

"Wait — partner. There's one more thing." He went to the front of the wagon and climbed up onto the seat. "When Uncle Bill had his wagon built, he had them make a secret compartment."

Bill leaned down and a moment later came up with three 14 inch sacks, each about as round as a silver dollar.

"There's close to a thousand dollars here. Pa dipped into it to buy supplies about a month back."

"This the uncle you were named after? Uncle Bill. The sea captain?"

"Oh — yes."

"You sure you don't want to use this money to go back home?"

"I'm sure. We all wanted to go to Texas. Now it's only me — but I don't want to turn back."

"Let's do this, then. Hand me one roll, and we'll put it in the saddlebags. Then if we tie the other two together, end to end, you could wear them under your shirt around your waist. They'll be a might heavy, but they could help strengthen your legs."

Bill agreed and climbed down. He handed one bag to Ethen while using pig ties to attach the other two bags. He pulled his shirt out of his pants and secured the bags of coins around his middle.

"You sure this is a good idea?"

"Nobody will suspect you of carryin' money if we get held up. And besides, it's your money."

"No, it's our money now, Ethan."

Ethan took one of his feet out of one of the stirrups. The lad sprang up in and settled up behind Ethan on the bedroll. Bill had his Winchester across his lap and held on to the lead rope to the packhorse.

"Texas, here we come," Ethan said with a smile, and Bill managed a small grin.

"I was told about a town on the other side of The Little Red," Ethan said over his shoulder to Bill.

"That's Texas, isn't it?"

"Not quite. There's the Little Red, the Arkansas, and the Ouachita all between us and the real Red River -- and Texas."

"Isn't the Ouachita mountains?" Bill asked." We have to go through them, don't we."

"Yep. Let's hope maybe we can make it to Little Red today."

They stopped to rest the horses three hours later. They climbed down, and Ethan went to pee in the bushes. When he got back, Bill decided he needed to do the same.

"I'm surprised at you, Bill," Ethan called when the boy was out of sight.

"Why?"

"Boy your age should be eating everything in sight. My Ma said she thought my legs were hollow. She never could fill me up."

"I'm fine. I eat want I need," Bill said, coming back. "Hope I'm don't turn out sickly like my folks."

"I wouldn't call them sickly — but you're going to have to grow you some real muscles if you plan on farming."

They had a little bite before continuing their trip.

They rode on until dark was coming on. Through the trees ahead, they saw the rising smoke and the dancing flames of a campfire. Ethan pulled up.

He cupped his hands around his mouth and called out, "Hello, the camp!" He paused and continued, "Two riders. Have Arbuckles, beans, and ham t' share!"

"Who are you?" came a rough-sounding voice somewhere in the trees.

"Ethan Andrews and my partner — Bill Cooper." Ethan whispered to Bill, "How old are you?"

"Twelve," the boy said.

"Bill's twelve. We're lookin' for a blacksmith t' fix a busted wagon wheel."

"Come ahead on!" the voice call after a pause. "But come easy and keep your hand away from your guns!"

15

"Here we come," Ethan called back.

They rode through the trees to find a wagon sitting beside a big fire. Ethan helped Bill to the ground and stepped down himself. Ethan took off his gun belt and hung it on his saddle horn as a sign that they came in peace.

A grizzled man in his 40s, wild salt and pepper hair, stepped out behind them a trapdoor Sharps .50 in his hand. He carried a '51 Navy Colt in his beaded belt. The .36 caliber pistol had originally been a cap and ball revolver but had been converted to take cartridges. He lowered the rifle as he approached.

"It's gonin' t' take a blacksmith or even a wheelwright to fix your problem," the man said. Every time he spoke, his gravelly voice sounded like he was almost out of breath — but he never was.

"That's what we thought," Ethan said. "We were hopin' to find one in the next town."

"The Little Red's about a quarter of a mile on south of here. There's a town there. They call it Seary. Not much, but I think they do have a blacksmith."

"I guess we'll find out."

"You mentioned Arbuckles?"

"In my saddlebags."

"Get 'em out and come on over by the fire."

Ethan turned back to the paint, loosening his cinch first and then fishing out his can of coffee, two cups, and what was left of the ham wrapped up in cheesecloth.

They approached the older man's fire. He was dressed in buckskins and sporting a beard long past the need for a trim. "What's your story?" he asked.

Ethan sat the coffee can and the ham on a rock by the fire and offered his hand.

"Ethan Andrews. This is Bill Cooper."

"Gilmer Thebadeau." They shook hands all around. "Where you pilgrims headed?"

Ethan glanced at Bill as he said, "My family raised horses. They'll all gone now, but I figured I could do that. Bill wants t' give farmin' a try. We're thinkin' Texas."

CHAPTER 5

"Thebadeau," Ethan asked, making coffee over the open fire. "I've known a couple of Thebadeaus. You from Louisiana?"

"You'd think so. Most of us are, they tell me. But I'm Canadian. Kind of lookin' for family — more or less. Spent a year fighting in the end of your Civil War when I found three of them. So after it was over, I decided me and the military were better goin' our own ways."

Ethan poured three cups of coffee.

Gilmer savored the drink for a bit before he began again.

"Met a cousin during the war. He had six toes on his left foot. Said there was a lot of strange things in parts of the family. Kind of cooled my interest. Still, I had to go. Been as far as New Orleans — met a bunch of folks with the same last name. Some didn't think I was any kin — and I'd have t' agree. They hunted alligators t' eat.

"There was this one woman," Gilmer continued, "— they called her the widow Thebadeau. She'd buried seven husbands. None of them was named Thebadeau. But she was. Ugly as a stump. Don't see how she ever got even one husband, much less seven."

He took a second drink.

"Had a Chippewa wife for a while. That was before the war.

Wanted t' be a mountain man in those days. Made me a jack of many trades — smithin' ain't one of them, though. She left me. Said I talked too much."

"You seen anyone leading a couple of mules without a wagon?" Ethan asked.

"That's strange thing t' ask. Last night there was, a couple of scalawags rode up. I didn't like the look of them. They weren't up to no good — I could tell that. I run them off and made sure they crossed the river b'fore I called it a night. Why do you ask? They your mules?"

"Belonged to Bill's parents. Two men came by while Bill was out fishing t' get some supper. They stole everything they could, including their mules. They shot up his water barrel on the side of the wagon just for the hell of it."

"I was right about them, then."

"Seems like it. Might be a good idea to keep a watch out tonite. They could come back," Ethan said. "I'll trade-off with you if you like. Want first watch or second?"

"How about me?" Bill asked, getting to his feet.

"No slight intended, partner, but you've not had any experience at this kind of thing."

"How am I going to get experience without doin' it myself?"

"Tell you what, you can stay with me during my shift. I show you what we do and what we watch and listen for."

"All right," the boy said, taking his seat.

"That OK with you, Gilmer?" Ethan asked. "You don't really know us. So you think you can trust us to be awake while you sleep?"

"I'm a light sleeper," the grizzled man said. "I'm also a pretty good judge of character. You two seem straight t' me. But if you don't mind, I'll take the first watch."

"Whatever you say," Ethan said. "This is your camp."

"Then unload your packhorse, and I'll start some supper. One thing I am is a pretty good cook."

"You wouldn't have to be much to be better than me," Ethan said. "I'm afraid I made Bill sick last night."

"Cookin' is one of the best things I do. After we eat, try t' get some sleep. I'll wake you in a while."

Ethan nodded.

❦

Gilmer woke Ethan and Bill a bit after midnight.

"Everythin' quiet — best I can tell."

"We'll make sure it stays that way," Ethan said as he and Bill got up, each took a cup of warm coffee, and headed out to the woods.

Later, as the three were havin' breakfast, Gilmer said, "I had an idea last night. I got a spare wheel on my wagon. Why don't we take it and my mules back t' get your wagon? We could get you across the river and into that town. You got money t' buy new mules or horses."

"A little," Ethan said without even a glance at Bill. "I thought if we had t' buy horses, I use my packhorse as one."

"Then we might be able t' get you two back on the road for good."

"You wouldn't mind doin' all that?" Bill asked.

"My Ma used t' call it earnin' stars fer my crown. I don't know about that, but this is somethin' I can do. I ain't headed anywhere in particular, and I ain't in any hurry to get there."

"That would be a great help, Gilmer. We'd sure be obliged."

"Then let's do it. We're burnin' daylight."

❦

It was afternoon by the time they reached Bill's wagon.

"Son of a bitch," Gilmer said.

"What?" Ethen was looking around.

"That wagon. You know what that is?"

"A wagon," Bill said.

"It's a Studebaker. 'Bout the best wagon made."

"My Pa's brother bought it for us. He's a ship's captain. He wanted us to have something solid if we were goin' all the way to Texas."

"Well, he sure as hell did right by you. Let's get this thing fixed."

The three got Gilmer's spare wheel off the travois. They had rigged the Indian carrier between the two mules. Within an hour, they had the spare on the wagon, the mules harnessed up, and were ready to go.

"We ought t' make it halfway back t' my wagon by dark," Gilmer said.

"Mind if we wait a bit?" Ethan asked.

Gilmer noticed Bill standing between the graves of his parents and nodded his head. "We got time," he said.

They did make it halfway back to Gilmer's wagon before they stopped for the night. Ethan and Bill took the first watch that night.

"One of the things you don't want to do," he explained quietly to the youngster, "is look back at the fire. Our eyes get used to the dark, and looking at the light causes you to lose that for a while."

Bill understood and got the hand of moving quietly while staying in whatever shadows the moon or stars were casting. Ethan also told him about the Big Dipper and how you can always find your directions at night by locating it.

The next day they paused, and both Gilmer and Ethan checked Gilmer's campsite before ridding in. Ethan moved the stake and the lead rope from his packhorse. They left Gilmer's wagon where it was and headed on toward the river.

Crossing the Little Red was easy. The water flow was slow and gentle. An hour later, they came to the town. Gilmer was right about Seary. The place was just getting started. The blacksmith there said it'd take two days to fix the wheel. But told them about two men trying to sell a pair of mules. The blacksmith said he passed on the deal because he had no money. He did have a workhorse he was glad to sell to Ethan and Bill. He said it was the first cash he'd held in his hand in over a year.

They planned to take the new animal back across the river when the wheel was fixed, and they could return Gilmer's spare wheel and his mules.

The young blacksmith started working on their wheel. Ethan and Gilmer sat on a bench on the porch of a saloon drinking beers the second day while Bill had a bottle of sarsaparilla.

"We sure owe you for your help, Gilmer," Ethan said.

"Oh shaw," he said. "If we don't lend a hand when we can, who'll help us out when we need it."

Both Ethan and Bill liked the sentiment.

"But," Gilmer continued, "I've got another question for you two," Gilmer said.

"Shoot," Ethan said.

"How'd you feel about adding this ol' coot to your partnership?"

Ethan and Bill exchanged looks.

"You want to go to Texas with us?" Ethan asked.

"Why not? Been there b'fore. When I left Lousiana, I trailed a herd from Ft. Worth up t' Kansas. Come back through east Texas jest a while back. Figured I was headed back t' Canada. But I don't believe I'm as interested in goin' home as I first thought. Been thinkin', Ethan you know horses, Bill you're goin' t' try farmin' — well, I know cattle. A place that did all three might do better than turn a profit. What do you think?"

Bill and Ethan studied each other a moment before Bill stood and offered his hand to Gilmer. "I say, welcome, partner."

Ethan shook hands on the deal as well.

"But," Bill asked," could you do me a favor?"

"Don't see why not? What can I do?"

"Take a bath. There's that creek we passed as we came into town."

Gilmer took a whiff of himself and laughed. "That's another reason my Indian wife left me. But I think it's about time. I might even shave some of this fur off of me," he said, rubbing his scraggly beard. "I just hope I don't kill the fish."

They all agreed and laughed together.

CHAPTER 6

The partners headed off the main road toward the river. They had clean clothes from the wagon and Gilmer a new set of buckskins he bought at the general store. Bill patted his money bags tied under his shirt, looking at Ethan.

"If it's all the same to you two, I'd like to practice a little with this pistol Ethan loaned me. I can do all right with a rifle — Pa taught me. But, a pistol is something sort of new to me."

"Good idea," Ethan said. "Your practice and that ought to keep trouble away while we at least scare the fish."

Gilmer laughed. "Sure, why not. Jest be sure not t' aim at the river."

"I'll use that old tree there," Bill said, pointing to a thick black walnut.

"You get good enough t' hit some of the green walnuts still on the tree, and you'll be a right fine shot."

"I want to be quick, too," Bill said.

"Don't worry about that," Ethan said, stopping and removing his gun belt. "Everybody talks about being fast — but I've seen too many fast men shoot into the dirt or miss their target completely — and end up dead. Being accurate is more important. Know what you're shooting at and be steady enough to hit it."

"He's right," Gilmer added. "You'll live a lot longer that way."

The two older men trooped off through the weeds as Bill checked Ethan's pistol and took aim at a large knothole.

❧

By the time Ethan and Gilmer got back, Bill knocked a green walnut off with every shot. He was reloading as his partners approached.

Gilmer looked totally different. He had a deep cleft in his now clean-shaven chin and a pair of dimples in his cheeks. His hair wasn't even, but he had used his knife to hack it much shorter.

Ethan looked pretty much the same, except for the clean clothes and the mustache he had decided not to shave.

"What do you think?" Ethan asked, stroking his newly covered upper lip.

"I like it," Bill said. "Fits you."

"How about me?" Gilmer wanted to know.

"Without your voice, I wouldn't know it was you, Gilmer. But you clean up pretty well. You might want to think about making that a habit."

Gilmer laughed and ran a hand through his hair. "I sure feel lighter."

They watched Bill take his next six shots and score with each one.

"You're damn good with that thing," Ethan said. "We ought to get you one of your own."

"I think I'd like that," he said, shucking the spent shells.

"You do know that you should only carry 5 shots don't' ya'?" Gilmer asked. "Six is OK for practice — but you don't want t' be walkin' around with your hammer on a live shell. You could bump into something, even drop your pistol — and that damn thing would go off."

"Oh," Bill said, studying his smoking revolver. "I'd never thought about that. I wondered why there were only 5 shots in it when I started."

"Get yourself a bath," Ethan said. "I'll clean the gun. When you're through, we can go check on how the wheel's coming — and see if we can't find you a pistol and a rig of your own."

"Deal," Bill said, handing the revolver to Ethan butt first. "How's the water?"

"Jest right," Gilmer said. "Course it had t' get through a few layers of dirt and sweat b'fore I felt it."

They laughed, and Bill headed for the creek.

They pulled back across the river the next day with the new wheel and trailing the new harness horse. They had plugged and sealed Bill's water barrel.

At Gilmer's camp, they let the mules out to graze with the new horse and Ethan's packhorse. Ethan and Bill gathered wood while Gilmer started a fire and supper.

"How's your belly ache?" Ethan asked Bill when they were returning with an arm full of wood.

"Better. Kind of comes and goes."

"Wish there had been a doctor in that town," Ethan said, putting his wood down near the fire. Bill added what he had gathered to the pile.

"We'll find one," Gilmer assured them.

"Oh, I'll be all right. Don't worry about me," Bill insisted.

They had a good supper and sat back talking about the kind of place they should be looking for when they got to Texas.

"We'll need good grazing for the horses," Ethan said, looking over at Gilmer, "and for the cattle."

"Most of the cattle'll be wild, you know," Gilmer said.

"My guess is the same for the horses. We'll need a coral for breaking."

"And a house," Bill added. "I don't think we ought to be planning to live out of the wagons by next winter."

"He's got a good point there," Gilmer said. "From what I saw when I come through there, there's plenty of trees. They call east Texas the piney woods. Less I miss my guess, there might be more trees than cattle or horses."

"Good," Ethan said. "Cause I figure we'll need not just a house, but a barn — and maybe even a bunkhouse for extra hands if we get to doing well."

"That's a thought," Gilmer said. "And a cook shack."

"Then we'll be talking about getting a stove?" Bill asked.

"Sound like we've got our work cut out for us. First of all, we'll need to find just the right spot. Then, if we're planning to make a go of this, we'll need a source of water."

"So we'll be looking for grazin' pasture, a place t' build on, not too far from a river or steady creek."

They sat in silence, drinkin' coffee as twilight approached.

"Another thing," Gilmer said, "Since that Studebaker wagon's heavier — cause it's better built, why don't we let the mules keep pullin' it. We can put the horses together t' haul my rig. It's lighter."

"That does make sense," Ethan said.

"What's the next town we should hit?" Bill asked.

"Well, there's Little Rock — but if it's all the same to you two, I'd just as soon avoid that place. I had a little trouble. Had t' shoot a fella. He was a braggart and a stupid drunk. He was also slow on the draw — but the law there was his brother. I think they'd like to throw me a necktie party."

Ethan said, "I haven't lost anything I need to look for in Little Rock. You, Bill?"

"Not a thing," the boy said.

"We still got t' cross the Arkansas somewhere near there. I figure we can find a crossing downstream about a half day from Little Rock. Now, that's if you're sure you're all right, Bill, and don't need a doctor right away, the next biggest place we'll come through is called Arkadelphia. Foothills of Ouachita Mountains," Gilmer said. "It's a growin' place. There's a salt mill there — and a hotel. More than one doctor, I'm sure."

"Arkadelphia," Bill repeated, letting the word roll around his mouth. "I think I'll be fine. Let's not go out of our way cause of me."

"The Ouachita River runs through it, and there's a lake nearby. Couple of different trails run through there. Not a bad little place, but it's not what we're lookin' for."

"It's still in Arkansas, isn't it?" Bill asked.

"Sure. We won't be in Texas for a day or two after that."

CHAPTER 7

The trio made good time without pushing the teams. They were still going up and down hills. There was no point in trying to overdue either the mules or the horses.

Half a day beyond the Arkansas, they paused for rest. Both Ethan and Gilmer climbed down and watered nearby trees. Bill, as usual, did his business off in the bushes. Then, when he had been gone longer than either of his partners thought was right, they got up to go look for him.

"That's far enough," Bill called from behind an old pine tree. "Get me that light blanket on the top of the chest in the wagon," he said. "Bring it back and drop it here — then go away."

Neither Ethan nor Gilmer understood what was going on, but they shrugged and went to the first wagon. Ethan found the blanket and handed it to Gilmer, who took it over to the tree.

"Drop it on the ground and go back to the wagons," Bill said, still out of sight.

Gilmer did as he was told, and Ethan saw their youngest partner come around and grab the cloth before retreating out of sight.

"You got any idea what's up?" Gilmer asked.

"Not a one."

A minute or two later, Bill emerged from behind the tree with two corners of the blanket tied in a knot over one shoulder. He looked like a Roman in a toga, Ethan thought.

"First things first," Bill said, stopping about halfway between the wagons and the tree he'd hid behind. "My name's not Bill — it's Bell. Mariah Bell Cooper. And I'm not a boy — I'm a girl — starting to be a woman."

Ethan's and Gilmer's mouths dropped open.

"All those pains of mine — and —," she looked down at her toga, but no words came out. "My mother told me all about it. It's natural — and it's who I am."

"Well," Gilmer finally managed to say, "that sure as hell 'plains a lot."

※

There were so many questions neither man knew where to begin.

"It was Mother's idea," Bell said when she finally approached Ethan and Gilmer. Pa thought it a good idea, too. Traveling as a boy was easier. Mother cut my hair, Pa got me some clothes, and they called me Bill. They were afraid of what might happen to me if anyone found out I was a girl."

"They weren't wrong," Gilmer said. "So, what do we do now?"

"Bill — ah, Bell — are we still partners like we agreed?" Ethan asked. "Have you had second thoughts about contacting your uncle and going back to Norfork?"

"Nothing has changed as far as I'm concerned," she said. "How about you."

"You have my word and my handshake," Ethan said. "I don't go back on either."

"Well, me, too," Gilmer said, wanting to make sure he wasn't left out.

"And we'll treat you like a boy if you like." Ethan looked at Gilmer, who nodded his head.

Nothing was said for a few moments as the trio stood looking at each other.

"I started my monthly," she said, blushing. "I didn't think that was possible for at least another year."

"And you bellyaches?" Ethan asked. "They were cramps?"

"Yes," Bell said, hanging her head. "I should have known."

Ethan and Gilmer understood.

"Than what do we do?"

"If we're still partners," she said, "we go on with our plans. Nothing has changed there. I will have to have my privacy — when I need it."

"No question about that," Ethan said. "But we got to deal with the fact that things aren't the same."

"We can all work on it — including the way you two talk around me."

Ethan and Gilmer both swallowed and nodded their heads.

"Aren't there any of your mother's dresses left in the trunk?" Ethan asked, gesturing toward the back of the wagon."

She closed her eyes a moment and then said, "I tore them up to wrap around Pa."

"Then let's get on the road," Gilmer said. "We need to get to Arkadelphia — get you some proper clothes."

"And — things a lady needs," Ethan added.

"A lady?" Bell asked.

"And that means you're goin' t' change your last name," Gilmer said. "You're too young t' be Ethan's wife — but you could be his kid sister."

"Mariah Bell Andrews," Bell said slowly. "I can do that. Is it all right with you, Ethan?"

He looked sad for a moment before he said, "I had a sister — once. I'll take care of you like I should have taken care of her."

Ethan studied the ground a moment more and then looked up at Bell, saying, "It's also time to put all our cards on the table, don't you think?"

Bell agreed. She turned to Gilmer and said, "We got some money. There's more than what's in Ethan's saddlebags." She patted the roll of coins around her waist. "Not counting what we've spent on the new horse and harness — there's about a thousand dollars."

"Whew," Gilmer said. "That's good. I ain't said nothin' about the

$800 or more in gold I got hidden in pouches at the bottom of my water barrel. All t'gether, it seems like we have what we need for a good start in Texas."

They all grinned and then laughed out loud.

"No more secrets, partners," Ethan said, and the trio shook hands all around on that pledge.

"I still want my own pistol," Bell said, "and a holster for it."

CHAPTER 8

Arkadelphia turned out to be everything Gilmer said it was. Friendly folks, new buildings going up, and a few established ones which seemed to be thriving. They stopped at the first livery they came to.

A livery owner who was all muscles and teeth greeted them.

"Lookin' for a place t' park your wagons — feed your horses and mules?" he asked, wiping his hands on a leather apron.

"We are," Ethan said, still in the saddle. "But we've come a piece and don't want to lose anything."

"Town Marshal Volbert Fankhouser live in that house right across the road. He's a retired army major and don't take no nonsense from anybody. I sleep in the back of the stable — and you know how horses are to strangers and noises in the night. Your wagons'll be safe here."

"I like what I hear." Ethan leaned down and offered his hand, saying, "Ethan Andrews."

"Lafe O'Bannon," the blacksmith said. A freckled-faced boy about 7 came out of the stable. "This is my son, Crockett."

"Mr. Andrews," the boy said.

Ethan motioned to the first wagon. "My sister Bell. Partner Gilmer Thebadeau's driving the second wagon."

The blacksmith walked down and shook hands while introducing himself to Gilmer.

Ethan stepped down from his saddle, and Crockett took the reins. O'Bannon came back but spoke loudly enough for Gilmer to hear.

"We'll park your wagons right here beside the stable."

Ethan helped Bell down. Neither the blacksmith nor his son said anything about the strange way Bell was dressed. Gilmer wrapped his reins around his wagon brake handle before joining the group carrying a leather bag in one hand his Sharps in the other.

"Headed fer Texas?" O'Bannon asked.

"We are," Ethan said.

"Most folks comin' down the trail the way you come are. We like Arkansas — but everybody's got t' choose their own place. How long you figure t' be here?"

"You have a hotel here?"

"A couple. There's the Zilker far end of town — and The Occidental. Right down the street — middle of town. Owned and run by our mayor, Wendal Omey. He'll fix you right up."

"We thought to take a rest here. A couple of days at least," Ethan answered.

"Make yourself t' home. We've got some good places t' eat, 3 generals stores, and half dozen saloons."

"Closest store? My sister needs some new clothes. We had a fire, and all her washing got burned up."

"That would be Painskey's. Across th' road, first corner on the next block," O'Bannon pointed.

"What's your rate?" Ethan asked.

"Dollar a day for each wagon and team. Feed, water, exercise in the back coral."

Ethan handed O'Bannon a five-dollar gold piece. "Let's start with this. We'll be by from time t' time. Settle up before we leave."

"Pleasure doin' business with you folks."

Painskey's was well stocked, and Hall Painskey, the round-faced proprietor, was quick to help. He called his wife, Alida, to help Bell. They went into the back room.

Ethan picked out a new 5 inch barreled Model 3 with an ivory grip for Bell. He also bought several boxes of shells. Hall pointed out a saddlery further up the street as a place to get Bell a holster.

New Levies were Ethan's goal, along with a couple of fresh shirts. In addition, Gilmer got himself some new boots.

After a half-hour, Bell emerged in a simple but nice-looking dress. She whirled around to show it off to Ethan and Gilmer.

"Brother's will never tell ya'," Gilmer smiled, "but I can say it very becomin', Bell."

"Thank you, sir," she said, making a small curtsy.

"I'll bring the rest of your things to the hotel," Mrs. Painskey said to Bell.

"Thank you."

Ethan paid the bill and said they'd be back for some food and canned goods in a day or so. The Painskey's were pleased and seemed to be nice people.

※

The Occidental was a fancy name for a relatively straightforward but unglamorous hotel. The place was clean and orderly. There was a dining room right off the lobby.

The balding mayor, Wendal Omey, was also the clerk.

"We need three rooms," Ethan said, "One for Mr. Thebadeau, the two side by side for my sister and me."

Omey dipped a pen in the ink well and offered it to Ethan, who nodded toward Gilmer first. After signing, Gilmer asked, "You got a reliable bank in town? I need to deposit while we're here."

"First Arkansas," Omey said. "Two blocks down on your left. Solid, safe — never been robbed."

"There's always a first time," Gilmer said under his breath to Bell, who giggled. He took his key, but instead of going to his room, he went back out the front door and left for the bank.

Ethan signed in and gave the pen to Bell. She signed and accepted the offered key from Mr. Omey.

"Up the stairs, then towards the front. Both rooms look out on our main street."

"Thank you, sir," she said.

"There's a bath at the back. If you like, we can have it filled right away."

"Please do," Bell said and started to turn away. But she turned back and said, "Oh, Mrs. Painskey will be bringing in some boxes.'

"I'll have them delivered to your room," the clerk promised.

Ethan looked toward the dining room. "When do you serve supper?"

"About two hours," Mr. Omey said. "And if I do say so, my wife is the best cook in town."

After they inspected their beds, Ethan met Bell in the hall.

"While you soak, I think I'll go find a place to have a beer. We can meet back here for supper. And," he said, making sure she was paying attention to him, "You should write your Uncle Bill. He deserves to know his brother's dead — and his sister-in-law. Are there folks on that side of your family who need to know?"

"No one."

"Tell your uncle about Gilmer and me. Tell him we're going to Texas as your father wanted. And you can say you'll write when we get settled. He'll want to know. Family's important. It seems to me your uncle truly cares about you."

"You are right, Ethan. I will do that. I know his address. But he could be at sea and might not get my letter for a few months."

"Still, he'll want to know."

Back at the front desk, Ethan asked the owner, "Where's a quiet place to have a beer?"

"If it's a quiet place you want, I'd recommend the Broken Wheel."

That brought a slight chuckle from Ethan. "Sure. Where is it?"

"End of the block. This side of the street. Now, remember, you asked for a quiet place, not a fancy saloon."

"Quiet is what I'm looking for. Tell my partner where I am when he comes back, will you?"

"Yes, sir."

The Broken Wheel seemed to be a sign of some sort to Ethan as he entered the rather plain saloon. A mulatto of about 20 was sweeping what looked to be an already clean floor. There was a woman behind the bar as Ethan stepped over. There were no other customers.

"I asked for a quiet place to have a beer. I see your mayor was correct."

"A beer. Coming up. She took a clean mug off a folded cloth at the end of the bar and placed it under a spicket. She handed him the brew, saying, "Here you go." Ethan placed a nickel on the polished bar. The brew was cool and tasted fine. Ethan nodded his head.

"Good. This place is better than the broken wheel we had up the trail."

"Sometimes, even at night, we don't even get that busy," the slender woman said. She was maybe 30. Curvy in all the right places, with shiny dark hair piled up on her head. She was appealing in a black v-neck dress which didn't invite stares.

"Ethan Andrews," he introduced himself.

"Vella Keifer," she said, offering her hand.

"How do you keep it open?" Ethan asked.

"Barely," she said. "What else can I do. We were going to Texas, then my husband found this place and thought it would be an easier way to make a living than farming. Used all our money to buy it."

"Things didn't turn out like he expected, I assume."

"They did for a while," Vella Keifer said. "I mean, we weren't getting rich, but we came out ahead at the end of each month." She sighed and closed her eyes for a moment. "This was Roman's business. My husband. He ran it. Til' a drunk shot and killed him one night."

"I'm sorry to hear that."

"Thank you. They hung the drunk — who didn't even remember killing Roman. But my husband was still dead — and so is the Mort Combs."

"That the drunk — Mort Combs?"

"Yes. That's all we ever knew about him. A cowboy who couldn't handle his liquor. It killed both my husband and him, too." She cleaned the spotless bar. "I should have sold this place to the chubby drummer, Widell Twiggs, yesterday. But we paid 2 thousand. Twiggs was offering $800. I couldn't do it. I've been struggling a year now — but I can't let it go." After a moment of silence, she said, "I don't know why I'm telling you all this. I'm sure you have your own troubles."

"Don't we all. But sometimes it is good to talk about it — especially to a stranger who is not judgemental."

"Well, thank you for listening," she said. Ethan crossed the bar and took a seat at a table.

Gunshots were heard from down the street.

"I thought this was supposed to be a quiet place," Ethan said.

"Usually is — or I'd be doing better business."

Ethan got up and hurried outside. A minute later, he was back. He sat back down, finished his beer, and ordered another one.

"Mind havin' one with me?" he asked.

"Thanks. I don't mind sitting with you," Vella said. "But the only thing I have left to sell — ain't for sale."

"I'm only looking for company. Think that's my partner taking care of something down the street. He should be here in a bit."

"You're not worried about him?"

"No. Gilmer can take care of himself very well."

CHAPTER 9

The First Arkansas Bank was a brick building. There were bars on the windows, and the place projected strength.

Gilmer put the deposit receipt for the partnership money in his shirt. As he turned to go, 3 cowboys had just entered the bank. One wore a duster and looked around at Gilmer and the two women in line for the other teller. The last cowboy closed the door and locked it. That was when Gilmer cocked his Sharps at his side pointed down at the floor. The third cowboy stepped over to the bank guard, who was dressed in a dark suit and railroad conductor's hat. He was holding a shotgun across his chest.

In a quick move, the last cowboy shoved the thin blade of a long knife into the guard's belly. The cowboy in the duster pulled out a short-barreled coach shotgun from under his wrap.

"Don't nobody move, and nobody gets hurt," the one with the shotgun said as the robber by the door drew his revolver. The leader swept the twin barrels of his weapon from Gilmer to the two women.

Gilmer raised his rifle with one hand and fired. The close quarters were instantly filled with white gun smoke. Gilmer then yanked his revolver and shot through the fumes at the robber by the door. Then,

Gilmer caught the cowboy with the long knife, thumbing his pistol twice more.

Everyone except Gilmer covered their ears from the exploding gunfire and dropped to the floor. The .50 caliber round had struck the robber with the shotgun in the chest threw him across the room. Gilmer's first pistol shot hit the robber at the door square in the center of his body. He fell against the door he'd just locked. The following two shots hit the knife killer — one in the shoulder and the other in the ribs.

As Gilmer began checking the bodies, horses were heard taking off at a gallop outside the bank.

The bank president emerged from his office with a small four-shot nickel-plated revolver. The women were squatted against the wall, and the two tellers were still crouched inside their cages.

Gilmer shucked the spent shell in his rifle and loaded another as he reached up and unlocked the door. The plump bank president looked over the bodies and the blood on the floor. Hurried footsteps came thundering up the boardwalk outside. A sturdy man in his mid 40's stepped in holding a Colt Peacemaker and wearing a brass Town Marshal's star on his vest.

He noted the silence in the room and the fact that the man in buckskins had a Sharps in the crook of his arm as he reloaded a revolver.

"Is anybody hurt, Mr. Winkle?" Marshal Volbert Fankhouser asked the bank president. The two tellers stood and came out to help the two women get to their feet.

"Looks like Lionel," banker Winkle said, stepping over to the bleeding but unmoving bank guard.

"What happened?" the marshal wanted to know.

Gilmer looked up as he put this revolver back in his belt. "I jest made a deposit. And then these three come in planning a withdrawal. I didn't think they had anything in the bank."

Winkle stood and said, "Lionel's dead. It appears they stabbed him."

"The one on the floor nearest him had what I think you call an Arkansas Toothpick," Gilmer said. "He stabbed the guard while the one by the door locked it. And this one," indicating the one in the duster, "pulled out a shotgun."

"You shot him with your Sharps?" the marshal asked.

"Seemed like the best thing t' do at the time. My pistol was still in my belt."

❦

At the Occidental's dining room that evening, Gilmer told the tale of the attempted bank robbery.

"I thought that first shot was your Sharps. Nothing else sounds like that," Ethan said. "I was ready to run to the bank when I heard the other pistol shots. I also saw two fellows hightail it out of town from in front of the bank."

Ethan and Gilmer sat with Bell. She wore a new dress, and her hair was combed differently, and she looked delighted.

"When I saw the marshal running towards the bank, I figured you had taken care of whatever had happened."

"What th' hell — pardon me, Bell — what th' heck was you doin' that was so important?"

"Talking to a woman in a quiet bar. If you'd gotten back in time, the clerk would have told you to join me at The Broken Wheel for a beer."

"Broken Wheel?"

"Yes. Isn't that both ironic and funny?"

"Don't know what — iron — onic — means — but I guess it means 'a little funny.'"

"It is," Bell agreed.

Gilmer sat back and produced a new corncob pipe from his vest. "Miss Bell," he said, "you mind if I smoke?"

"Of course not," she smiled. "But I'd like to change and make you my uncle. Uncle Gilmer."

"Uncle?"

"Well, since Ethan is my brother — you can be my uncle."

Gilmer laughed. "Never been anybody's uncle that I know of. Uncle Gilmer. I kind of like it."

"And how did you spend the afternoon?" Ethan asked Bell.

"Had a long soaking bath in clean water — not Little Red River water. When I got back to the room, the boxes had arrived from Painskey's. I tried them all on. What do you think of this one?"

"It's lovely," Ethan said.

"Not much t' travel in, is it?" asked Gilmer.

"It's my Sunday-go-to-meeting dress. I also bought myself some pants and work shirts. I'm ready for travel or work, too. But I want you two to see all of my new dresses."

"How many are we talkin' here?" Gilmer said, taking a puff from his pipe.

"Only five — but I still want you to see them."

"We can go up to my room," Ethan said to Gilmer, "while she changes next door. She can come in when she's ready."

They had fresh pecan pie for dessert. When Mayor Wendal Omey came back to their table, Ethan said, "Our compliments to Mrs. Omey. She's as good a chef as you said. What's our bill?"

The balding man held out his hands palms up, shaking them. "Your money's no good in Arkadelphia. Banker Winkle said so. He sent out word that anything you wanted or needed while you're here — the bills are to go to The Arkansas Bank."

"Ain't that nice?" Gilmer said.

"Mr. Winkle said the whole town would have lost a lot of money if those robbers had been successful."

"They can't say they've never been held up, no more," Gilmer grinned.

"No, but thanks to you, Mr. Thebadeau, it didn't lose a dime. Marshal Fankhouser said you sure made a mess of the first jasper with your Sharps."

"It tends t' do that," Gilmer said, drawing on his pipe again. "Guess I taught all of them not to go around tryin' t' steal from other people."

"The Marshal says there were two more waiting outside, but they got away. He doubts they'll be trying something like that again. At least not around here. I hope you enjoy your stay." The mayor/hotel owner walked away with some of their empty plates.

"We'll need to see about a holster for you, Bell," Ethan said. "That's for tomorrow."

"And I'd like to look around the other stores in town," she said. "Now that I'm not a tomboy anymore — there are other things I'm interested in."

"Gilmer, what are you going to do?"

"Jest look around, I guess. I ain't much of a town guy, but I do make the best of it while I'm here."

"Well, meet me for a beer later."

"At The Broken Wheel?"

Ethan laughed. "You'll like it in spite of yourself."

CHAPTER 10

Bell wanted a cross-draw holster. She was left-handed and wanted to wear it high and not too far away. The saddle maker had one Bell liked. The man had to punch an extra hole in the belt for it to fit. Her new pistol would have its handle covering her belly button, Ethan guessed, but he didn't say so.

The saddle-maker had gotten word from the banker, so Ethan and Bell left without paying a penny.

She went off shopping on her own, and Ethan took her rig back to the hotel. She didn't want to wear a gun in town.

That afternoon Ethan found Gilmer already at The Broken Wheel, enjoying a beer at the bar, his foot upon the foot rail. The lady poured a beer for Ethan as soon as she recognized him walking in. He asked her to have one on him and come sit back at the table.

She brought a beer for Gilmer and one for herself.

"Vella Keifer," Ethan said, "one of my partners. Gilmer Thebadeau."

"Everybody in town knows the name," she said, offering him her hand before she sat. "He's our hero."

"That don't seem t' fit me right," Gilmer said, quickly downing his beer. "I did what needed t' be done. I ain't nobody's hero."

"Like it or not, you're our hero."

Gilmer made a face and stood. "I think I need to do some walkin'."

"Well, don't stay away," Vella said. "Come back and drink some more. I'll love sending the bill to Banker Winkle."

Left alone, Ethan and Vella talked easily.

"What were you and your husband going to do in Texas? Farming, did you say?"

"Yes. At least, that was the plan. I knew it wasn't going to be an easy life — and I don't know if I ever really believed Roman wanted to be a farmer. But — I was in love. And I know hard work, and I'm not afraid of it."

"What did your husband do — before you married?"

"Roman had been an officer in war — a captain. He was always proud he'd served under General Bragg. But after the war, he had trouble finding what he wanted to do. He studied law a while but got bored. Then he was a school principal in Knoxville, Tennessee. That's where we met. I was a teacher, too. But Roman didn't like being a principal. He switched to organizing wagon trains. That he was good at — but it gave him the itch to go to Texas. That's what he told my father. I don't think Daddy ever believed him."

"You think you were going to be a teacher in Texas?"

"Not unless we were close to a town. I thought I'd be a farmer's wife."

Two rough cowboys came in. The mulatto young man went up to them.

"What can I get for you, gentlemen?"

"Hey, look, Slade. A half nigger serving as a barkeep," the shorter of the two said to the other, who was dustin' off his hat on his pants.

Vella got up quickly and went behind the bar.

"I'll take care of them, Odel," she said, and the younger man went to the back room.

"Now that's more like it," the short cowboy said. He leaned over Vella until she asked again, "Beer? Whiskey?"

"Whiskey," the tall one said.

Vella got out two glasses and poured them both a drink.

"Leave the bottle, pretty lady," the rude, short one said. "And you stay, too."

"I have other things to take care of," Vella said politely, moving her arm before the cowboy could grab it. She walked back over to where Ethan sat, bringing him another beer.

"I do think I see why you might want to sell," he said quietly.

The bat-wing doors burst open, and Gilmer stood there trying to adjust his eyes from the sunlight the darkness of the saloon.

"I found our mules, Ethan. Livery up the street bought them real cheap from a couple of hard cases."

The shorter cowboy drew his pistol and fired at Gilmer. His shot went to the floor before Ethan jumped to his feet, filled his hand with his Schofield, and fired. He hit the left-handed gunman in the ribs. The lead tore through his abdomen, and the shooter fell to the floor, dead.

The taller cowboy had also fired toward Gilmer but whipped around and fired a shot at Ethan. Then the gunman fired another round at Gilmer before running out the doors. The saloon was filled with white smoke. Ethan fired into the haze at the fleeing man without being able to see his target.

Odel came on a run with a baseball bat in his hand. Vella slowly rose from her knees off the floor. There was no more shooting.

"Mrs. Vella, is you all right?" the mulatto called.

"I'm OK, Odel," she said, steadying herself into a chair.

Ethan stepped over the dead cowboy and kicked the pistol away from him. Then he went to the front doors. Gilmer was sitting with his head down and his hands on the back of his head. There were two bullet holes in the door frame near him. Outside, a horse raced away.

"Gilmer?" Ethan asked, helping his partner to his feet.

Gilmer rubbed the back of his head. "I'm OK," he said a little too loudly, having been temporarily deafened by the close quarter's gunshots. "They missed me, but the second one knocked me on my ass, and I banged my head a'gain th' wall."

Ethan helped Gilmer to a chair, and Vella stood and went to the bar. She returned with a bottle of whiskey and a couple of glasses.

Marshal Fankhouser came in holding his shotgun. The average-sized man had an air of authority and seriousness about him.

"Vella?" he called out.

"Over here, Marshal," she answered, sitting beside Gilmer. Odel brought over a cool, damp bar cloth for Gilmer. Gilmer nodded his thanks and applied the fabric to the back of his head.

"Who was shot?"

"The cowboy who started it. He's on the floor by the bar."

The marshal walked over and knelt, seeing that the shooter was dead. The marshal came back to the table and recognized Gilmer.

"You again, Mr. Thebadeau?"

"He was the target, Marshal," Ethan said. "He just stepped inside, and that cowboy drew on him."

"Who shot the cowboy?"

"I did. Ethan Andrews. I'm Gilmer's partner."

The marshal sighed and lowered his shotgun. He looked back at the body. "Flem Staker. Was there another man with him? Taller?"

"Yeah, he shot at Ethan and me," Gilmer said. "Son of a bitch kicked me into the wall as he ran out.

"That would be Slade. The Staker brothers. I guess it was Slade doing a Pony Express mount on his galloping horse that I saw out front." To Ethan, the marshal said, "You just got yourself a reward. Both of them are wanted — dead or alive. One thousand dollars each. 'Course, you'll have to wait til' t'morrow for me to get approval back from Ft. Smith. Judge Parker will want to be sure it was Flem. I think I can get you a bank draft by noon."

"We'll be around," Ethan said. "I think we have some horse-trading t' do."

"Me, too," Gilmer said, putting down the wet cloth from the back of his head. "How long b'fore you're free Marshal?"

The undertaker, a lanky man, dressed in a black suit and wearing a top hat, pushed through the gathering crowd outside the saloon and entered.

"There's Neil Gully, now. He'll take care of the body. I've got about an hour's worth of paperwork to do — including a telegram to Ft. Smith. Why?"

"Jest t' sure nobody else gets shot, I thought you might want to be at Orland Mowan's — say in about an hour. We have a little tradin' t' do, an' he ain't pleased about it."

"I'll try to be out that way," the Marshal said.

Ethan turned to Vella. "Having second thoughts? Would you be interested in selling your saloon for less now?"

"More inclined than I've ever been. But I don't think that Widell Twiggs is still around anyway?"

"You mean the fat fella' in the plaid vest and big gold watch-chain?" Marshal Fankhouser asked. "He's still around. I saw him at breakfast at the Zilker."

"Maybe he'd be willing to up his price," Ethan said.

CHAPTER 11

Gilmer led both of the horses they'd been using to pull his wagon over to the Orland Mowan livery on the west edge of town. Marshal Fankhouser was leaning on a hitching rail directly across from the corral when Gilmer arrived.

Orland Mowan was a short, taut man with a full beard of reddish-brown hair. His hands were knotted up in fists, one on each hip. Gilmer handed the reins of Ethan's packhorse and the bay they had bought in Searcy. The owner kept shaking his head.

"I figure this is about an even swap," Gilmer said.

"Nothin' even about it. Those two horses are worth about what one mule is worth.

"But we both know those mules were stolen, and you got them very cheap."

"What I paid for them is my business."

When the liveryman wouldn't accept the reins of the two horses, Gilmer pulled open the gate and led the horses in. Then, he began removing the harnesses from the horses and putting them on the mules.

Mowan looked over at the lawman.

"He's stealin' two mules from me, Marshal. You're seein' this."

"What I don't see is how someone can steal stolen property."

"I didn't steal 'em."

"But you knew they were stolen when you bought the pair, didn't you, Orland? This isn't the first time you've pulled something like that. And we both know it." The Marshal stood and ambled over to Orland Mowan.

"Mr. Thebadeau saved whatever money you had in the bank yesterday."

"I heard that. But it don't give him the right t' walk in here and take my mules."

"But are they your mules?"

"I bought 'em. I have the sales receipt."

"Signed by one of the Staker brothers?"

"It's still a legal document."

"Want to test that in Judge Woodrun's court?" Marshal Fankhouser asked.

Gilmer walked out of the coral leading the mules. He didn't close the gate, but Mowan hurried over and did.

As Gilmer walked away with the mules, Mowan said, "We elected you as marshal. We could unelect you, too."

"Tell your friends," Fankhauser said before he turned away. "If you have any friends."

Ethan caught up with the drummer waddling out of Marsh's Mercantile. He had a wide grin on his flabby cheeks as he looked at his order book in his hands. Ethan stopped the man before the two collided. The sales agent tipped his bowler hat.

"I beg your pardon," Twiggs said. "I don't mean to take up more of the boardwalk than I should."

"No damage done," Ethan said. "Are you Widell Twiggs?"

"I am, sir. Should I know you? I have a memory for faces and names. It's important in my line of work."

"No, we've not met. What is your line, if you don't mind my asking?"

"Not at all." He produced a business card from a vest pocket and gave it to Ethan. It read: Widell Twiggs, Traveling Sales Agent To The World. It had an address in a St. Louis hotel at the bottom of the card.

"Ethan Andrews — horse breeder, rancher — pioneer," Ethan said as the men shook hands.

"What can I do for you, Mr. Andrews? My clients are usually businessmen of some type — mercantile to dress shops, gun stores to bootmakers. Occasionally, I deal with ranchers and farmers — but usually only those which are large businesses by themselves."

"You made an offer to buy The Broken Spoke saloon the other day."

"I did. From what I hear, there was a killing there only a while ago."

"You keep an ear to the ground, it seems?"

"Part of the trade. I need to know what's going on."

"Well, the reason I'm looking for you, Mr. Twiggs, is because I've acquired a stake in The Wheel. So I thought if you're still interested in buying the saloon, we might be able to come to an understanding."

"Ah," Twiggs said, hooking his thumbs in his vest.

"That shooting certainly makes the property less attractive."

"Does it? Or does it make it a place of interest?" Ethan questioned. "Are you married, Mr. Twiggs?"

"Married." The question threw the salesman. He didn't know what this had to do with The Broken Spoke.

"Twice, as a matter of fact," Twiggs admitted. "My life on the road is not very conducive to matrimony. Why do you ask?"

"I believe you are tired of stagecoaches, a different hotel every couple of days — and are interested in an established business — in a good town — where you might like to live. But a business with growth potential — and one you could pick up on the cheap."

"I won't deny anything you've said, Mr. Andrews. But what do you have to offer?"

"You were willing to pay $800 for The Broken Spoke the other day. The lady who owns it wasn't interested."

"Correct?"

"Fifteen hundred dollars would still be a good buy for the place.

Look at its location. And the new interest it's now gained. I'm sure 15 hundred would still be within your budget."

"A thousand five hundred? No, no. Maybe I'd be willing to come up a little from my original offer — but not that high."

"What would you consider? Twelve hundred?"

"I could see myself going to an even thousand —, but that would be as high as I would go."

"A thousand," Ethan said, rubbing his chin. "That still seems low to me."

"That's my offer. Take it or leave it," Twiggs said, spreading his feet apart in a firm stance.

"We could be close — but — no. A thousand isn't enough. The lady's husband originally paid 2 thousand. So, no. I guess we can't do a deal after all."

Ethan turned and stepped back down into the dirt. He had gone less than five steps when the salesman called, "All right, 12 hundred."

Ethan stopped thought a moment and turned back to Twiggs. "Cash on the barrelhead."

"Done," he said and spat in his hand. Ethan spit in his, and the two men shook hands. "I'll have calls to make today, and I don't carry that kind of cash on me."

"I'll meet you in The Broken Wheel — tomorrow — 2 o'clock. I'll sign over the deed," Ethan said.

"I'll be there," Twiggs said and headed towards the bank.

CHAPTER 12

Ethan returned to The Broken Wheel. There was the biggest crowd he'd ever seen in the place. Many of those there pointed out the blood spots on the floor near the bar. Vella and Odel were both busy.

Ethan took the only vacant table and sat for about an hour while the customers thinned. Vella finally joined him and brought a fresh beer when she came.

"Don't forget to put that on my tab for banker Winkle," Ethan said.

"Oh, I won't," she smiled.

"I have a proposal for you, Vella?"

"Proposal?"

"I think we can help each other out."

She sighed. "I'm listening."

"How about selling The Wheel? Have you changed your mind? Say for even thousand dollars?"

She slowly nodded her head, saying, "OK."

"But I don't know what I'm going to do after that," she said.

"Are you still interested in Texas?"

"I haven't thought about it," she said.

"Vella, I see you as a level-headed woman. Would you sell The Wheel to me for that bounty money the marshal has promised?"

"You want to buy a saloon?"

"This one."

"Why? Aren't you on your way to Texas?"

"What if I bought The Wheel and gave you a way to get to Texas?"

"How would that work?"

"I find myself in need of a wife. You could use a new life."

"Marriage? Ethan, you don't know me, and I don't know you."

"You've been married before, Vella. I have a teenage sister. She needs a mother — or at least an adult woman to show her the way to womanhood. And I'm not talking about an ordinary marriage — let's call it a business arrangement. I wouldn't expect anything from you unless you somehow decided I was someone you truly wanted to live with."

Vella sat back in her chair, overwhelmed by what Ethan had said.

"A business marriage?"

"Well, in so many ways, a marriage is a business. Both partners need to be headed to the same destination. I know it's supposed to be a lot more — but here we are — two people who need someone and something — in common. Why not this? Maybe it will become more — in time. As I said, I wouldn't expect anything else from you. Anything," he emphasized. "You and my sister — she's twelve, by the way — can sleep together, and you'll never have to worry about my expecting more." He let her think about it a few moments before he said, "We — Gilmer and my sister — are going to Texas. We plan to start a ranch/farm. Start a new life for us all. If you like it — it could be the new life you want."

"Just like that. We get married."

"Doesn't have to be in a church. I'm sure there's a judge somewhere around."

Vella closed her eye. She put her head down on her folded arms on the table. Ethan said nothing. He just let her think.

It was a full minute before she sat back up, looked around the saloon, and finally turned to Ethan.

"Yes," she said. "I'll sell you The Wheel — for one thousand dollars. And — and I'll become Mrs. — what's your last name, Ethan?"

"Andrews. Ethan Andrews."

"This may be the craziest thing I've ever done."

"Then we're starting out even."

"Not that it makes any difference, but my name is Vella Keifer. Vella Gartaman Keifer."

"Mrs.Gartaman Keifer — I try very hard to be a man of my word. And I'll do my best to be a good husband to you — whatever that turns out to be."

※

It was 3/4 past 11 the next day when Marshal Fankhauser arrived with the reward telegram from Judge Parker. The lawman saw that both Ethan and Vella were dressed up.

"Something going on?"

"Was," Ethan said. "Judge Woodrun married us about 10 this morning."

"Married?"

"I'm selling The Wheel," Vella said, looking at Ethan. "And we're going to Texas."

"I see," the marshal said, although Ethan guessed he did nothing of the sort. He put the telegram on the bar and asked for a pen.

"Odel," Vella said, "there is a pen and ink on the desk. Would you get it for the marshal?"

"Yes, ma'am."

When Odel returned with the pin and the ink well, Marshal Fankhauser dipped the pen and wrote his name across the bottom of the telegram. He returned the pen to its holder, which Odel took back to the office, and handed the sheet of paper to Ethan.

"Garnet Winkle is expecting you. I warned him yesterday."

Ethan took the telegram and said to Vella, "I'll go cash it and be right back."

After Ethan was gone, the marshal asked Vella, "This is kind of sudden, isn't it?"

"It is, Marshal. But after the shooting — I knew it was time for some major changes in my life."

"I wish you luck, Vella. If there's ever anything I can do for you, you know where to find me."

"Thank you, Volbert. I appreciate it."

Ethan was back in less than 20 minutes. He crossed to the bar and counted out the one thousand greenbacks to Vella on the bar. She picked up the money and handed the folded deed to The Broken Wheel to Ethan.

He slipped the deed into his coat pocket as he asked, "Vella, are you packed?"

"Yes. It turns out there's not that much I really want to take with me. Everything fit into one trunk. It's up in my room."

Ethan turned to Odel, "Would you give me a hand?"

The mulatto young man came around the bar, ready to follow Ethan up the stairs without a word.

Before Ethan moved, he asked his new wife, "You want to travel in that dress?"

Vella looked down at her dress and then back to Ethan.

"No. I'll go change. I'll call when the trunk is ready."

She went up the stairs by herself.

A few minutes later, she appeared at the top of the stairs in another dress — one, unlike anything she'd ever worn in the saloon. It was light blue cotton and plain. Her hair was down and swept over one shoulder.

Ethan and Odel went up for the trunk as Vella passed them coming down the stairs. The two men returned with the worn travel trunk.

Gilmer came in with Bell. The young lady was dressed in trousers and a work shirt. Gilmer was back in his buckskins.

"Parked the Studebaker out front. I'll go back and get my wagon. O'Bannon is hitching it up for me now."

Vella smiled at Bell. "You certainly got changed in a hurry. But, first, I wanted to tell you what a lovely dress you had on for the ceremony."

"Like I told Ethan and Uncle Gilmer, it's my Sunday-go-to-meeting dress. I showed it to them the other night. I didn't expect to need it for some time. The wedding was all the reason I needed. I got changed so quickly because I wasn't sure Uncle Gilmer would wait for me too long," she smiled.

"You are making all of this very easy for me," Vella said.

"I tried to put myself in your spot and couldn't imagine how you were feeling. This has been so quick. Ethan tried to explain it to me — and I know he's doing this more for me than for himself. But I've read stories where love is like that."

"Bell, you need to know that Ethan and I aren't in love. Our marriage is a — business arrangement. He needs a wife —"

"He certainly does," Bell said. "And he believes I need someone, too."

"— and I need to restart my life — if I can. Ethan said you needed — a woman around."

"He's right?" Bell lowered her head.

"He said you were becoming a woman and — well, I've been through that. I also made all the mistakes that go along with that. Maybe I can help you avoid some."

Bell twisted her mouth as she nodded her head. "He's right."

"I can't imagine how all this feels to you," Vella said.

"I trust Ethan — and Uncle Gilmer. If anything is all right with them, it's more than fine with me."

"Including me?"

"Especially you, Vella," Bell said. "I know we're both going to have to get used to each other — but I'm not worried. If you and Ethan aren't in love — you're surely taking a big chance on each other. My guess is you'll find he's the kinda man any woman would want."

"Wish I could feel that way."

"You will. I'm sure of it."

CHAPTER 13

Gilmer had withdrawn the partnerships' money from the bank and thanked Mr. Winkle for his generosity.
"We're still in your debt, Mr. Thebadeau. If you or your partners are ever back this way — you will always be welcome."

"Much obliged," Gilmer said.

When Ethan came into the bank, banker Winkle was waiting for him. He cashed the reward telegram before the two partners headed back. Ethan stopped at The Broken Wheel while Gilmer went to the stables to get the wagons.

At precisely 2 o'clock, Widell Twiggs pushed open the door of The Broken Wheel checking the time on his pocket watch. He put the timepiece away, looking up and spotting Ethan and Vella along with Odel.

"Mrs. Keifer," he said, tipping his bowler.

"It's Mrs. Andrews — as a few hours ago," Vella said. She held up her left hand and displayed her new wedding band.

Twiggs saw the trunk on the floor. "I see. Congratulations, Mr. Andrews. You did acquire an interest in The Wheel — and more."

"I did," Ethan said. Then, turning to Bell, he said, "And this is my sister Bell."

"Miss," Twiggs tipped his hat again. To Ethan, he said, "Shall we get down to business?"

The two men stepped over to the bar. Twiggs pulled a stack of 100 dollar bills out of his pocket and began counting them out on the bar. Finally, he finished saying, "Twelve hundred."

Ethan handed the salesman the deed to the property.

"Keys?" Twiggs asked?

Ethan turned to Odel, who walked over and laid two keys on the bar. Twiggs picked them up as Vella joined them.

"Twelve hundred," Vella said. "You bought it for 1,000 from me."

Ethan took 2 one hundred dollar bills from the stack of bills and handed them to his new wife.

"There. I wasn't going to cheat you."

"I want to make a change in our — arrangement. Odel goes with us."

Odel looked up, surprised.

Ethan asked, "Odel, you want to come to Texas?"

"I'll go anywhere Mrs. Vella goes."

Vella handed $100 to Odel.

"What's this for, ma'am."

"All the times you didn't get paid — and for standing with me."

Ethan looked at Twiggs. "You'll need a bartender."

"Check with the Nugget," Vella said. "Offer $50 a month to Luke Lindhoff. He'll come for that — and he knows where everything is around here."

"Luke Lindhoff," Twiggs repeated the name.

"Slicked back blonde hair and a thin face," Vella offered.

"We'll be gone in a few minutes," Ethan said. "The Broken Wheel is yours, Mr. Twiggs."

"It will become The Full House," Twiggs said assuredly.

Ethan looked at Vella. "Can you drive a team?"

"It's been a few years, but yes."

"Good. So can Bell. Why don't you and Bell take the first wagon." Ethan turned to Odel, "What can you do besides tend bar, Odel?"

"Whatever needs doing," he replied.

"Then let's load the trunk, and I'll take you down to meet Gilmer. You can ride with him."

Gilmer was pulling up behind the Studebaker when Ethan and Odel approached.

At the second wagon, Ethan said to Gilmer, "We've got an addition to our party. Gilmer Thebadeau, meet Odel —, "Ethan glanced at Odel, "— I don't know your last name."

"Smith," the mulatto said.

"Odel Smith," Ethan finished.

"Climb aboard, son. We're burnin' daylight."

Ethan unhitched the Paint from the back of Gilmer's wagon and swung into the saddle. He rode up beside Bell and Vella, who were settling into the seat of the first wagon.

"Let's see how far we can get before we have to camp."

"We're not getting to Texas today?" Bell asked, taking up the reins.

"Not quite. Tomorrow we'll cross the Red. But we're starting too late in the day to make it that far. So let's do the best we can."

Ethan rode on, Bell popped the reins, and the first wagon began to move. A moment later, Gilmer's wagon was in motion, too.

"Tell me about yourself," Gilmer said to Odel.

Reluctantly, Odel said, "I was born a slave."

"Don't mean a damn thing no more," Gilmer said. "Hell, I'm a bastard. I have no idea who my daddy is. Don't think my ma was ever sure either."

"My father was the head overseer at the plantation. That's why I'm half white."

"Don't know anybody who ever did get a chance to pick their parents," Gilmer said. "All that counts is what you make of yourself. Where we're goin', it's goin' to be up to each of us to do it all, or it won't get done."

"I'll do my share — and more," Odel said.

"Good man," Gilmer said. "Can you drive a wagon?"

"Yes, sir."

"Let's stop this 'sir' business. I'm Gilmer. Here you drive, and I'll tell you about the Thebadeaus."

❦

Ethan found a good camping spot not far from a stream. He hobbled the paint and helped Bell and Vella unhitch their team. Odel pitched in, and Gilmer could tell the younger man knew horses and wagons.

Bell gathered firewood, Odel put out the iron stakes and the cooking pot rail. He located the coffee pot and the other pans. Gilmer brought out the beans and some beef they'd gotten from Painskey's General Store first thing after the ceremony in Judge Woodrun's court. They were well stocked.

Ethan was rubbing down the paint when Odel came over and started working on the mule teams. He brought a bucket and filled it with water from the stream. He saw that each animal had their fill.

Vella took over the cooking when she redid some of Gilmer's work, and he saw she knew what she was doing. So he turned his attention to the coffee.

After everyone had eaten, Ethan asked. "How was it? Traveling today."

No one had any complaints.

Bell and Odel took on the task of cleaning the dishes. While the sun set, Ethan asked Odel, "You ever stood watch?"

"I was in the army three years."

"Take a Winchester here and take the first watch. I'd do second, and Gilmer, you okay with last?"

"Makes no nevermind t' me."

"I'd rather use Gilmer's Sharps instead of a Winchester. I'm more familiar with it."

"Fine," Gilmer said, reaching for his rifle propped against a wagon wheel. He reached in his pocket and gave Odel a fist full of shells.

"After you are sure of me," Odel said, "I don't mind taking mid-watch. It's likely easier for me to get back to sleep than either of you."

"Good man, Gilmer said."

"When is my turn," Bell asked.

"We're going to leave you ladies out — if you don't mind."

"I can still do my part," Bell insisted.

"Nobody questioning that. But I'd rather do it this way. You ladies sleep in the Studabaker, and the men will use the second wagon. All right."

"It's part of being a woman — they don't realize our work is never done," Vella said as she motioned to Bell made up their beds in the wagon.

"Aren't you and Ethan — ?" Bell started to ask but didn't know how to finish the question.

"Not tonight," was all the answer Vella would give.

CHAPTER 14

Ethan blinked a couple of times and sat up on his blanket under Gilmer's wagon. Gilmer snored away inside the wagon above. Odel handed Ethan a cup of hot coffee. Ethan took a sip and reached for his boots which were upside down on stakes he'd driven into the ground.

Ethan brought his half-empty cup to the embers of their fire. Odel sat down across from him.

"There's someone out there," Odel said. "Five to 6 hundred yards east of us, I think."

"Doing what?" Ethan was awake and alert now.

"Nothing. Made a camp. I never saw any fire. Could have hidden that, or it could have been a cold camp.

Ethen thought this over as he checked his pistol and then his Winchester. "Strange," he finally said.

"I thought so, too. But whoever it is, he didn't try to approach. He must have seen our fire and the canvas of the wagons."

"Somebody going the same way? Or someone keeping an eye on us?" Ethan's questions were rhetorical. "Thanks, Odel. I'll let you know if there's something more. Get some sleep."

Odel nodded, leaned Wilmer's rifle against the back of the wagon, and stacked the shells Gilmer had given him beside the weapon. Then, hearing Gilmer's snore, he decided to make his bed out in the open on the other side of the embers. He did add a few sticks to the hot goals to make sure the fire wouldn't go out.

Ethen walked out about 50 yards and stood his post in the darkness. After a while, he walked a slow circle around the wagons. He returned to his original position and peered into the blackness while listening to any sounds. All he saw and heard were normal and natural sights and sounds.

When it was time to wake Gilmer, he told his partner about what Odel had said.

Gilmer drank a cup of coffee, checked his Sharps, and repocketed the shells before he stepped out into the dark.

Ethan saddled the paint and rode out as Vella and Bell started some breakfast.

He found signs of a cold camp, just as Odel had suspected. But whoever it was had moved on. Southwest towards Texas, he observed.

Back at camp, he told Odel he'd been right and complimented him on his observation skills. The women were curious as Odel told them what he'd told Ethan and what Ethan had passed along to Gilmer.

"Should we be worried?" Bell asked.

"No so much worried as aware," Ethan said.

They packed up their camp and headed on down the increasingly worn trail.

Before lunch, they reached The Red River. It was nearly a quarter-mile wide at the end of the trail. The red sand and clay-colored the steady flowing water. The only building on their side was a shack where a middle-aged man and woman lived. Their business was running a hand-pulled ferry between the two sides of the river.

Hamp and his gaunt-looking wife Nan Newnhan — ran the Red River ferry. The friendly couple told them it was their son, Jude, who was on the other side. She collected 25 cents for each passenger, animal, and wagon.

Hamp was thin but muscled. They loaded Bell's wagon and her two mules along with Ethan and his horse for the first load. Ethan, Vella, and Bell all helped pull on the rope to move the load across.

Three freight wagons had pulled in to the south side by the time Ethan, the women, and their wagon unloaded on the other shore. The first of the freight wagons were loaded for the trip back.

There were three open buildings on the south side — two saloons and the third a blacksmith. Five other buildings remained but were empty. Each showed the signs of having been flooded. Even the open building had high water marks from when the river had overflowed its banks.

"We're in Texas at last," Bell said, standing in the wagon as she pulled up past the last building to await Gilmer and Odel.

"Sonny," Ethan said. "Not yet?"

"What? I thought the river was the boundary."

"It usually is," Ethan said, loosening the cinch on the paint. "This just happens to be the place that's still in Arkansas. They used to call this Fulton. I don't know what it is anymore?"

"Then when do we get to Texas," Bell almost pouted.

"In Texarkana," Vella said, forcing herself not to laugh. "The next town ahead. There's a road there called State Line. One side's Arkansas, and the other is Texas."

❦

Five miles further on from the ferry was Texarkana. The town was bustling and bigger than Arkadelphia. New lumber marked the most recent additions. Businesses ran from liveries to sign makers. Two brick banks stood facing each other across the road called State Line. The railroad station was only a block away. There was a single building sitting in the center of the road. The road split went around it. It was a brick and wooded post office.

As Bell's wagon pulled past the building to the western side of the road, Ethan turned in the saddle and said, "This is Texas."

They halted two blocks into Texas on an empty lot. They watered the animals and hobbled them in an open field. Ethan drew the short straw and stayed to guard the wagons while Gilmer led Vella, Bell, and Odel into Henriette'a Cafe. After the noon-time rush had passed, the place was still serving a good-sized crowd.

They took a clear wooden table, and a young woman was quickly there with a cart. She placed clean jars, a fork, knife, and napkin at each place. She paused when she saw Odel. She wasn't sure what to say or do for a moment.

"He's with us," Gilmer said evenly.

There was a section of the cafe across the room with an entrance through a side door. The few tables there were for negros. The sever there was black.

The young waitress at the group's table took a deep breath and said, "Water or tea?" The girl lifted two metal pitchers from the cart.

"Got any beer?" Gilmer asked.

"Yes, sir. I'll bring you one."

"Tea," Vella said, and Bell chimed in with, "Me, too."

"Water, please," Odel answered.

She poured the drinks all around and set the pitchers in the middle of the table before asking, "What'll it be? Chicken and dumplings are the special of the day."

"Special all around?" Vella asked to the agreement of all.

"I'll bring your plates and your beer, sir." She left.

There was some grumbling from men at a nearby table.

Gilmer pulled out his knife and laid the blade down on the table. When he added his pistol, one of the men who stood up decided to sit down.

Bell drew her pistol and laid it on the table, too. She looked at Odel and then Gilmer. The older man just nodded.

Next, Bell brought out a leather-bound book she's been carrying.

"What's that?" Gilmer asked.

"Ma gave me this for a diary, but I couldn't find things to write about after a few days. I use it to draw and sketch on mostly." Bell had a short pencil tucked in the book and began doodling. "We're going to need a brand, aren't we?" she asked without looking up.

"Yep," Gilmer said. "Something that can't easily be changed."

Bell kept scratching on a page until the waitress returned with four bowls and a small plate of bread balanced in one hand on a tray. In her other hand, she had Gilmer's beer.

The girl moved away to clear a table where the grumbling men had left.

"What you got there?" Gilmer asked, looking over at Bell's book.

Bell put her spoon down from eating and opened the book for all to see. "What do you think of this as a brand?" What she had drawn was a capital A with the crossbar of the A having a line extending down.

"It's an A," she traced the letter darker, "and a T." She highlighted the crossbar and the descending line. A for Andrews — Ethan and me — and the T for Thebadeau."

"Ain't you fergettin' the newest Andrews?" Gilmer said, glancing toward Vella.

Bell cupped her hand over her mouth and flushed red.

"I'm so sorry. Of course, Vella. I'm sorry. I didn't even think of you."

Vella laughed and spoke while placing her hand on Bell's arm gently. "I'm still getting used to it, too."

"Looks fine to me," Gilmer said, pushing the book back over to Bell. I think we need to check with Ethan."

CHAPTER 15

Later, when they were finished eating and returned to the wagons, Ethan liked Bell's idea she showed him for a brand.

"After I eat," he said, "we can check with that blacksmith over there," he indicated a smithe across the road and a few buildings down. "See if he can make it and how long it would take."

"I think we need to arm Odel, don't you, Gilmer?" Ethan asked.

"I figure we can find a gun store," the older man said. "Odel, you ready?"

"Fine by me."

Ethan turned toward Henriette'a Cafe.

"Get the special," Vella called. "You won't regret it."

Ethan nodded and stepped up on the boardwalk. They entered the building. Vella turned to Bell and said, "Let's see your drawing. There's no reason we can't go see about this while he eats."

Together the women were off on their mission, keeping the wagons in view.

The gunsmith was Norwegian and spoke with an accent. He was of average height, rounded shoulders, and half-covered face with his mixed brown and gray beard.

"Come in, come in," he cheerfully greeted Gilmer and Odel. "Vat can I help you with?"

"Got a trap door Sharps?" Gilmer asked.

"Two of them." The gunsmith turned and walked over to the rifle rack. "One is brand new — straight from ze factory — and ze other is used — but I've reworked it myself. I had to replace ze firing pin and screws. Za trigger needed some attention, too. Now it is as good as ze new one — just broken in, as you say."

Gilmer looked at Odel and asked, "What's your pleasure?"

"The one that's been broken in will do me fine."

The gunsmith picked up the used rifle and brought it to the counter for Odel. Odel looked it over with an experienced eye. He sighted it out the window and nodded his head. "It's good for me."

"How about a pistol?" Gilmer asked.

"What are you carrying?" Odel asked.

"Converted '51 Navy Colt." Gilmer handed it to Odel, who hefted it and examined the pistol.

"Got any of those?" Gilmer asked the gunsmith.

"Not exactly. I have a '61 Navy," he said, producing the gun from under the counter. "But it's a .38 caliber."

"And the other bad thing about these," Gilmer said to Odel, "is that they're only 5 shots instead of 6 like all the newer ones."

"Here's the new Smith and Wesson top break." The gunsmith brought out another pistol.

"It looks like the ones Ethan carries," Odel said, examining the weapon.

"It is. Called a Schofield, but this one has ze longer barrel than Ethan uses."

The gunsmith opened the pistol by pinching latches on the back top of the barrel. The barrel assembly, including the cylinder, flipped forward.

"Zis here," the smith pointed to the prongs on the center rear of the cylinder, "ejects ze spent rounds for a quicker reload. I have it in .44 and .45."

Odel liked the way the revolver felt and smiled.

Gilmer then went into haggling with the man. He wanted 12 dollars for the pistol and 15 for the rifle. It took a quarter of an hour before they agreed on 22 dollars for the pair. The gunsmith had thrown in a cartridge belt and loop holster for the Smith and Wesson.

"We'll take the .44 pistol," Gilmer said, reaching for his money pouch inside his shirt, "and 6 boxes of cartridges for each."

When Ethan returned after eating, he saw Bell wave at him as she and Vella crossed the road from the blacksmith's shop. Ethan met them in the middle of the road.

"The young man said he could have it done by sundown," Vella said.

"While I was eating, I was thinking about how easy it would be to use a running iron to change the brand by adding a rocker or a box around. But, instead, we need to make it harder — put a star around it or something."

"I think I know how," Bell said with a smile.

Bell and Vella returned to the blacksmith with Ethan. The muscular man was in his late 20's with a square jaw. His name was Steem Griffin.

"The star is a good idea," he said to Ethan's request.

"How about this?" Bell asked, taking a stick and drawing in the dirt on the shop.

She drew a typical 5 pointed star with a single connected line. Then, kneeling, she erased the 2 pieces of diagonal lines at the top of the bottom 2 points of the star. Lastly, she drew a straight vertical line from the center of the horizontal line at the bottom of the top point.

"A — ," she said outlining the top point and legs down across the 2 sided points and the horizontal line at the bottom of the top point, "and T —," she redrew the horizontal and the vertical line down from its center."

"That's very good, Bell," Vella said.

"Clever," Ethan agreed, examining the drawing.

"Star AT," Steem Griffin said. "Yes. But it will take me until tomorrow to get it done."

"It would be worth the wait," Ethan said, getting an approving look from Vella. Then he asked, "You're a deputy sheriff?" Ethan saw a badge under the blacksmith's leather apron.

"Newly sworn — since the bank robberies," Steem said. "Sheriff decided he could use some part-time help and asked me to stay on."

"Robberies? You had more than one?"

"Two at the same time. The banks being so close made them a target, we figure. You heard about the one they tried in Arkadelphia?"

"We were in town when it happened," Bell said.

"Do you know who it was that hit your banks?" Ethan wanted to know.

"Outlaw named Slade Staker. I heard he lost a brother in Arkadelphia."

"That's what I heard," was all Ethan would say.

Vella looked at Bell, who had wrinkled her brow but said nothing.

"We chased them for a day," the deputy/blacksmith said. "But they had two sets of fresh horses waiting for them. I'll bet they're in New Orleans by now."

"Couldn't you take a riverboat and get there before they did?"

"No jurisdiction. In fact, the sheriff and half of us chasin' them were from Texas. This is Bowie County. The Arkansas deputies represented Miller County. Their sheriff was out of town. So, two different states — and we were in Lousiana when the Sheriffs decided not to kill our horses in a useless chase."

Nothing more was said for a few moments, and then Steem changed the subject.

"I can stable your mules and keep your wagons in the coral for the night if you a mind to stay the night."

"I suppose so," Ethan said. Then, looking at Vella and Bell, he said, "We could sleep in beds again."

Vella and Bell left to go back to the wagons.

As the blacksmith picked up a piece of steel and shoved it in the fire, he began pumping his bellows, and the flames glowed.

"Who the person is to talk to about land around here," Ethan asked Steem.

"What are you looking for?"

"We want to raise some cattle and horses."

"You talking dairy or beef?"

"I suspect we'll do a little dairy but mostly beef."

"Land around these parts are great for farming. Cotton is the biggest crop. There are more than a few dairy farms already around here."

"Then maybe what we need to do is to keep looking," Ethan said. "What's the going price per acre in these parts?"

"Anywhere 'tween 2 and 10 bucks and acre. Let me suggest you look around Mt. Pleasant. West southwest — a good six days or so. More meadows — lots of creeks — more pine trees than here. Land there for like 2 to 5 dollars an acre."

❧

Vella and Bell returned to the wagons. The 12-year-old grinned as she asked, "A hotel honeymoon?"

"Nope," Vella said quickly. "It's not part of our arrangement."

Bell still didn't understand. But before she could ask more, Vella said, "What we need to do is find Gilmer and Odel."

"Speak of the devil," Bell said, shading her eyes as the two men approached. Odel had the rifle in the crook of his arm and a new pistol in a new holster.

Ethan came back, seeing the weapons.

"You all set?" Ethan asked Odel.

"I believe so. Got me a rifle like Gilmer's and a pistol like yours."

"Good," Ethan said. "We're having a brand made — let's find a hotel.

"Sounds more like what we're lookin' for. We'll park the wagons and pick up the brand in the morning."

"I think I'll bed down in the wagon,' Odel said.

"You don't have to do that," Ethan assured him.

"I know," Odel said, "but I'd feel better."

"We'll get you for breakfast," Vella said, understanding.

As the partners headed up the street to find a hotel, Ethan said, "I think the land we want is further on west."

CHAPTER 16

The next few nights were spent on the trail. Finally, in the late afternoon and early evening light, they all pitched in and began to plan out what the Star AT would look like.

"We're going to need a barn — maybe two if we need to separate horse and cattle operations," Ethan said. "Corrals — I'm thinking 3 or 4." He drew out blocks for the barns and ovals for the corrals.

"How about a house?" Vella asked. "A well and a garden?"

"If we do this right, we could build a house — even two — but with the idea of connecting them and eventually making them all one big house."

"We could start out," Gilmer said, "with a single dog run house."

This two-sided house with a central breezeway or "dog run" was a basic structure with only two rooms — one on each side. By this time, the whole group understood that Ethan and Vella weren't going to be sleeping together. So one side could be for the women, and the men could take the other.

"But we're going to need a bunkhouse, cookshack, smokehouse — a pigpen, chicken coop," Gilmer went on. "How much land are we talking about?"

"Five hundred acres," Ethan said, "more or less."

"Do we have the tools we need for that?"

"Some. We could get by with what we have," Ethan said, sitting back. "But I suspect we're going to have to find a general store where we can pick up things like a log splitting wedge — and a couple more heavy ropes, block-and-tackles — some tents and tarp."

"How long will we have to cook over a fireplace?" This was Bell's question.

"Well, we'll have to start still living out of the wagons — but by winter, we should be inside. After that, we can see about ordering a catalog stove through the general store."

"The good thing is," Gilmer said, "it looks like wood won't be a problem."

"No, it won't," Ethan agreed. "But we're still going to be doing this the hard way — one tree at a time. We'll have to make everything from frames to shingles."

"You know," Gilmer mused, "if this operation of ours is going to be as big as we're talking about — we might want to consider a sawmill."

"That's one place I can help," Odel said, one of the few times he spoke. "In the army, I was in supply. My company built two sawmills and ran each of them for several months before we were relieved. So that's something I know about."

"Really?" Ethan said in surprise.

"That's a wonderful idea," Vella said. "What do we need to build one?"

"The Army ordered the whole thing — the steam engine, rods, big leather belts, gears, racks and — every bolt and screw," Odel explained. "I'm sure there are companies that sell all of it — together. But my guess is it will cost a thousand dollars — maybe more."

"A thousand dollars," Vella said. She thought a moment, then reached inside her blouse, between her breasts, and came up with a packet of bills. "Let this be my contribution. One thousand dollars."

Everyone in the group was in momentary shock.

"What," Vella said. "It's the money I got from the sale of The Broken Wheel."

Gilmer said, "Every general story has a batch of catalogs. I'll bet there's one for machines — and a section of sawmills."

"And it's going to take a lot of work, isn't it?" Vella asked.

"It is," Odel said, "— till it's built. Then we could make all the lumber we needed."

"That could turn into a business just by itself," Bell said. "There have to be others who will want lumber."

"That's the way we need to be thinking. Everything we do adds to the whole operation." Ethan turned to Gilmer, "You plan to get wild cattle?"

"There's still plenty of them running free. So I figure it's the way to start."

"How about dairy stock?" Bell asked.

"That we have t' bargain for," Gilmer said, pulling out his corncob pipe and lighting it. "But I'm guessing you planning to start with wild horses."

"We certainly don't have the money to buy any blooded horses. My mare, the paint, is excellent stock, and we should have some prime specimens in the wild. We'll have to develop our bloodlines."

"Won't that take a couple of years?" Vella asked.

"It will," Ethan answered. "So will building up a large cattle herd big enough to drive to market. And the garden and crops we can grow will have to be for ourselves for a while."

"And we keep growing all this time?" she said, thinking out loud.

"That's the plan. What money we have, we use sparingly. When we can do without, we do. But as soon as we have stock, horses, and cattle to sell — we should be in a pretty good position."

"The Star AT," Bell said. "I like dreaming big — it gives us something to work towards every day."

"How about hands?" Odel asked. "We'll need more than just us."

"I was thinking about a half dozen to a full dozen, to begin with," Ethan said. "And it will take time to weed out the workers from those who are little more than grub line beggers. We'll want men who aren't afraid of hard work."

"Your thinking of single men?" Vella asked.

"No," Ethan said, stroking his chin. "If part of the pay we offer is help men with families — well, even single men — start their own farms or ranches. There'll be plenty of available lands. Then, once we have our sawmill, we can turn out the posts, poles, studs, rafters, and siding to build whatever we need."

"Getting people out of their wagons and started on their own home would be very attractive," Vella said.

"So, where do we start?" Bell beamed.

"We find us the place we want. Then we horse trade and cattle trade to get some breeding stock, and next, go into the wild to gather horses and cattle."

"Mt. Pleasant should be about one more night and part of a day away if I'm right," Gilmer said.

"Everybody get rest," Ethan said. "We're getting closer and closer to Star AT."

CHAPTER 17

Their last night on the trail, when Ethan woke Odel for the second watch, he said, "Whoever has been following us is back."

This woke Odel quickly, and he got ready. Then, as he drank a steaming cup of coffee around the low flames of their campfire, Ethan said, "I think we should go out and pay him a visit."

"You go right, and I go left," Odel asked as he finished his coffee and hefted his rifle.

Ethan looked up at the moon, about a half-hour from setting.

"That will work. Let's take our time while we still have some light. Let's say we meet at his camp — about 500 yards out — just before the moon sets."

Odel nodded, and the two men moved out into the darkness but stopped to allow their night vision to evolve.

The hobbled horse snorted once at Odel who approached the animal slowly and without threatening. He managed to stroke the chestnut a couple of times before moving away, and the horse returned to nibbling clover.

Ethan came up through a stand of pines and walked softly on the accumulated pine needles. He stepped over to the sleeping man and moved his Winchester away by laying it in the grass. Odel quietly stepped up from the other side and leveled his rifle at the prone figure. Ethan leaned and slipped the man's Colt from the holster draped from the saddlehorn of the saddle he was using for a pillow. Then, with the man's weapons removed, Ethan polked the man in the back with his Winchester.

"Wake up," Ethan said in a loud, clear voice.

The man jerked and twisted in his bedroll, reaching for the pistol that was no longer there.

"Slowly," Odel said, letting the man know he was covered from two directions.

Around 20, maybe less, the young man sat up and raised his hands.

"What's your name?" Ethan asked.

"Woodie — Woodie Karten."

"Get up off your knees, Woodie," Ethan said.

The fellow did as instructed.

He was lanky, chiseled, and appeared to be tough. His bushy hair hung to his shoulders. He had chapped lips and birdlike eyes.

Ethan kicked the embers of his fire to life and tipped a part of a branch over until it caught fire and gave out plenty of light.

"What are you doing?"

"I was sleeping."

"When you're awake?" Ethen prodded.

"Drifting. Minding my own business."

"But you seem to be making it a practice of drifting along beside us. We've been aware of you since Arkansas.

"I ain't causin' anybody any trouble — especially you folks."

"That's a funny way of drifting," Ethan said. "Get up, Woodie Karten."

He kept his hands raised as he got to his feet.

"Why are you following us?"

"Nobody. I told you, I'm just driftin'."

"You're not fooling either of us," Ethan gestured to Odel, "or yourself. You had better come clean, or we're going to see if one of the branches here is strong enough to hold you up by your neck?"

"I ain't done nothin'?"

"You're trailing up — and it's not for our company."

"I ain't," he protested.

"Odel, get his rope, and let's see how strong it is?"

Odel pulled the rope off the saddle as Woodie watched.

"Find a branch — a strong one," Ethan said.

"All right. All right. I was followin' you."

"Because?"

Woodie wet his lips — and spoke, "Slade Staker."

"And why would Slade Staker want to know where we were?"

"He didn't tell me. He jest said t' foller you til you stopped and settled somewhere."

"How were you going to let him know?"

"He told me to come t' Jefferson on the Cypress. He said he'd find me there."

"When?"

"He didn't say. So I'm supposed to wait until he finds me."

"And why are you doing this? Are you in his gang?"

Woodie Karten was quiet and swallowed before finally saying, "Not yet. This is some sort of test, I think. To make sure I can follow orders and do whatever he says."

"What is it about being an outlaw that appeals to you?" Ethan slowly shook his head at the very concept. "The people you hang out with — the way they live — always on the run — the chances of growing old not very good? What is it?"

"My brother rides with Staker and his brother. I wanted to follow him."

"How long has it been since you've seen your brother?"

"A month maybe. Why?"

"What was he doing the last time you saw him?"

"Layin' around camp — getting ready to do a job."

"Where was this?"

"Outside Arkadelphia."

"Was it a bank job hold up they were planning?"

Woodie was shocked. "How'd you know that?"

"How many were in the gang — counting your brother?" Ethan had a suspicion.

"Five — counting Slade and his brother."

"Why didn't he want you to join the gang?"

"He said I didn't have any experience. So I told him I'd never get any if I didn't do something."

"When you met Slade, was he by himself?"

"Yes. Why. He come back to camp and picked up everything he had. That's when he told me that if I wanted to join the gang, I had to follow you."

"He didn't have his brother or yours — or the rest of the gang with him?"

Woodie knitted his forehead. "No. He was alone. What's all this about?"

"Slade's brother — Flem — and yours are dead."

Woodie's mouth opened, but he didn't have anything to say.

"Your brother was killed trying to rob that bank. His brother died the next day in a saloon shootout."

"How do you know that?"

"I killed Flem. A friend of mine killed all three of the men who tried to rob the bank."

Woodie dropped to the ground. His hand landed in the dirt on either side of him.

"But," Woodie seemed to plead, "They robbed both banks back in Texarkana."

"Did you see any of them?"

"No, but everybody was talking about it. They got a big posse to go after them. But Slade and everybody else got away."

"How about Flem? You heard anything about him — or your brother?"

"Nobody would know my brother."

"He wasn't there. He's buried up in Arkadelphia." Ethan let all of this settle in on the kid before he spoke again. "That's what you want? Is Slade Staker your hero, son? Is that what you want to be? Do you want to end up like your brother? What did his life amount to? What is your life going to be?"

There were tears in Woodie's eyes as Ethan emptied the shells out of the boy's Colt and then picked up his Winchester and leavered it until it was empty. Then Ethan pitched the pistol and rifle back to Woodie.

"You can go tell Slade to come looking for the Star AT — somewhere around Mt. Pleasent. Or take this chance and go find your brother's grave. You've got a lot of thinking to do. But, whatever you do, don't follow us anymore. Do you understand?"

Woodie was lost in thought, and Ethan said again, louder, "Do you understand?"

The would-be outlaw nodded his head.

Ethan and Odel returned to camp. Finally, Ethan went to bed, and Odel continued his watch until it was time to wake Gilmer.

CHAPTER 18

Nothing was said to the rest of the group in the morning. Packed up after breakfast, the Star AT troop moved on. They reached Mt. Pleasant before noontime.

The town's name came basically from the Caddo Indians, the ancient occupants of the area. They referred to the green rolling country of streams and lakes, endless forest, a warm climate, and bountiful rains as "pleasant mounds." Prehistoric peoples had built the mounds used as burial sites. When the Star AT wagons entered the area, it was known as Titus County. "Pleasent mounds" had been changed to Mt. Pleasant for the town and was less than half the size of Texarkana. It was a major stopping-off point for people and wagon trains on their way West.

Both wagons stopped in front of Hedgecock Mercential.

"We need tools for building and farming," Ethan told Gilmer and Odel.

"We'll water the mules first," Gilmer said.

Ethen went back to their first wagon. To Vella and Bell, he said, "We'll need tarps and tools — and that stove you talked about. We can move into a shelter when we get one built."

"We can see to that," Vella said as Ethan offered her his hand and helped her down. "What are you going to do?"

"I see a land office down the road. I'm going to see what's available." After helping Bell down, Ethan trotted on down the road. He ignored the multiple saloons and other thriving businesses and went straight to the false front building with "Land Agent" painted in bold black letters. Stepping down and loosening his cinch, Ethan stroked his mustache. He stepped up to the door and opened it before he went inside.

Vella and Bell were greeted by a pitted-faced man wearing a white apron. He was a bulky, pale-skinned man.

"Ladies, Abe Hedgecock," he said, dipping his head. "What can Hedgecock's do for you this fine day?"

"A stove," Vella said. "For cooking."

"Tarps, work gloves, and boots," Bell added.

"Tarps I have and can even cut to size," Abe Hedgecock said. "A stove will take about two weeks. I have catalogs you can look through and pick out exactly what you want. Right this way," he gestured to a counter with a stack of printed catalogs at one end. "Anything from pins to pianos," the man said. "He reached for the thick Montgomery Ward paper-bound book and opened to the section which covered kitchen and household needs.

Abe Hedgecock turned to Bell and directed her to follow him to the very rear of the store. Before reaching their destination, they passed tables of fabric and racks of dresses and skirts, pants, and overalls. The piles of tarps rose waist-high, and rollers of differing lengths covered the back wall.

"Oh, wow," Bell said. "I think I'll need Gilmer or Odel's help."

"Other members of your party," the store owner asked?

"Yes. We parked our wagons out front, and they're watering the mules. Is that all right?"

"Of course," the store owner said.

"I think both Uncle Gilmer and Odel should be in here pretty soon. Most likely even Ethan."

"Work gloves are over this way," the salesmen said as they walked through the story to a section where Levi's, boots, hats, and work gloves were kept. "Have the other members of your party see me when they arrive."

"I think I will," she said.

Vella had selected the stove she wanted. Mr. Hedgecock wrote up her order of a four cooking surface, double wood-burning box, bear feet model with an oven. Hedgecock helped her pick out stove pipes with elbow joints and a steepled tin vent.

Gilmer was looking at farming tools when a young man in his late teens and also wearing a white apron approached. "Bluford Hedgecock," he said with his hands clasped behind his back. "This is my father's store. What can I do for you?"

"Gilmer Thebadeau. I'm going to need to build some fences. I have axes and hatchets, but I could use a sit-down blade sharpener wheel, too."

"For your fence building, I believe you'll also find this useful. It's the latest thing. A posthole auger." He picked up the two-handled device and demonstrated how the metal clamshell ends could stab and collect a plug of earth and remove it. "Do this on two sides, and you'll end up with a perfectly round hole. Then dig as deep as you need."

Gilmer was entranced with the invention. "I'm going to want two of these."

"Yes, sir," young Bluford said, pulling an order pad from a front pocket and a pencil from behind his ear. He made a note on the sales pad. "I assume you already have a plow," he said.

"That we do. What we don't have are a couple of water pumps and pipes."

In the Land Office, a US government agency, Ethan looked at land maps on the early 40-year-old Littleton Tyner's office wall. Tyner wore sleeve garters on his starched collared white shirt. He was barrel-chested but short. He had a high forehead with thinning blonde hair combed straight. Clean-shaven Tyner pointed to patches of land southeast of Mt. Pleasent.

"There's a growing town this way — they call it Daingerfield. They were burned to the ground a few years ago, but they rebuilt it — just a little closer to the railroad. The top rate is 4 dollars an acre," Tyner said. "An abundance of woods and meadows. The Swauano Creek cuts through about halfway between here and there." The little man turned away from the map to Ethan.

"I think this would be ideal for raising horses. Cattle? I'm not sure. Cotton is still the cash crop in this part of Texas. The cattle ranches are way west and south of here."

"Well, we're looking at buying the machines for a sawmill."

"Oh," Tyner said, leaning back slightly. "What would you think about buying a used mill and moving it?"

"That's an interesting idea. Why would someone want to sell a sawmill? I'd expect that to be a solid business around here."

"It is. But when Edgar Rowling and his wife drowned in the flood last year, their boy, Davis, doesn't seem to want to stay or get the mill back up. He's waiting for someone to make him an offer. I'm sure you could get his land cheap."

"Where is that," Ethan asked.

"Right up here," Tyner tapped the map. "Straight south. Some people are trying to start a town down there — especially a 'Major' Pitts.' They'll call it Pittsburg. The Rowling place is a little north of there. Davis, the boy, might sell for less than a third of what a new mill would cost you?"

"Davis Rowling," Ethan said. "Thanks. How about this flooding? How often does that happen?"

"The old-timers called it a once in 50 years flood. I don't know. I haven't lived here but a few years. Let me draw you a map — help you can find the Rowling's place. "

"We'll go look at the land, too. If we find what we want, we'll be looking for about 500 acres."

"The flood didn't hit so hard a little east of there. So if you find what you like, I think with a down payment, any bank would take your mortgage."

A pistol shot rang out outside, and a bullet smashed through a pane of glass in the Land Office.

CHAPTER 19

Ethan had drawn his right pistol and dropped to his knees with the sound of the first shot. Then, with the glass breaking, he pulled his second pistol from his left holster and began making his way to the front door. Land agent Littleton Tyner had stooped over and opened a drawer on his desk. He came out with a .45 Colt and worked his way to the other side of the front door.

There had been no more shots after the first two. With a nod from Ethan, Tyner reached up with a gartered sleeve and opened the front door. Ethan stepped out on the boardwalk, ready to return fire. Tyner joined him standing on the other side of a boardwalk support post for the building's overhang.

Tyner lowered his pistol as he said, "The McMulliens! Wouldn't you know it."

Across the street, three men leaned against a hitching post rail. All had prominent brow ridges and full beards. They wore bibbed overalls over stained long john shirts, boots, and gunbelts. The one in the middle, seemingly the youngest of the three, late '20s, took three tries to holster his pistol.

"I'll be damned if you didn't, El," the eldest of the trio said, clapping the shooter on the back. This one looked to be in his mid 40's.

"The McMulliens cousins," Tyner said to Ethan. "A couple of times a year, they come to town, get drunk, fight, and bet on stupid things." The land agent stepped down into the road and approached the three men.

"Rollo," Tyner said to the oldest, "when are you three going to grow up?"

Through blurry eyes, Rollo looked up and said, "Hell, we're all grown. That's why I was betting Elridge could hit that knothole behind you in three shots. He done it in two. And as drunk as me and Ship, too. That's growed-up."

"Having enough sense not to go shooting off guns in town is childish," Tyner said. "You three are a public nuisance. If we had a lawman, he'd throw the lot of you in jail — every time you come to town."

"But you don't have no lawman, do you? And is there anybody in this whole town willin' t' take us on — even one of us?" This Rollo said to the growing crowd in the road. "You all know we don't mean no harm — and we pay for any damage we do. Shooting a knothole ain't nothing."

"No, but the first shot broke my window," Tyner said.

"And the second weakened this post," Ethan said, holstering his pistols.

"Looks fine to me," Rollo said.

Ethan gave the post a good kick, and it split in two, causing the overhang to droop.

"OK, I guess we'll need to pay for that — and your damn little window," Rollo said, digging into his pocket.

"The pole and the cost of putting it in," Tyner said.

Rollo produced several dollar coins, but he couldn't get them clear enough in his vision to tell one from another.

"Th' hell with it," Rollo said, repocketing his money. "You fix the window and the post, and we'll pay you next time we come t' town."

"You'll pay for it now," Ethan said, approaching the three men. "That's what a grown-up would do."

"Who in hell are you?" Rollo mumbled.

"A man," Tyner said, joining Ethan, "I was trying to interest in buying some land around these parts. But, I wouldn't blame him if he decided to move on and find what he's looking for somewhere else."

"Tell you what," Rollo pushed off the hitching rail, "if you can beat me." Then, he addressed the crowd, "Or any of us, we'll pay now — and leave."

"And leave your guns at home the next time you come to town," Ethan said.

"Beat you at what?" Gilmer said, stepping forward from the crowd.

"Anything. You name the game — shootin', fightin' — anythin'."

"How about a little rough-and-tumble," Gilmer said.

"Rough-and-tumble is our favorite game," Rollo said.

"And who's the best at it?" Gilmer asked, pitching his hat to the ground and dropping his pistol and knife on top of it.

"That'd have t' be Ship," Rollo said, pointing to the cousin on the end. "What do you say, Ship? Want t' show this ol' fart how it's done?"

Ship, who looked to be around 30, shook his head and forced his eyes wide open. He took off his gun belt and handed it to the shooter, El. Ship doubled up his fists, used one thumb to wipe the side of his nose, and started stepping around Gilmer.

"Rough-and-tumble," Rollo called out for all to hear. "No hold's barred. The first one to call 'Uncle' looses!"

Ethan had moved back but didn't see Vella and Bell, who each grabbed one of his arms.

"Stop this, Ethan!" Vella said.

"Look at the size difference between them — not to mention the age difference!" Bell said.

Ethan chuckled. "If you're taking bets, bet on Gilmer."

Ship lunged at Gilmer, trying to grab an arm full of wirey white-haired man. Gilmer stooped under the big arms and clamped his left hand over his right fist as he stepped behind Ship. Then Gilmer used the combined strength of both arms to slam a sharp elbow into the larger man's kidneys.

This got a groan from Ship as he staggered forward from the blow. When he turned back to Gilmer, both Ship's hands were to his back. Gilmer used the opportunity to throw a quick jab to the face and bloody Ship's nose. Gilmer also delivered a knee to Ship's stomach.

Ship whipped around from the attack, blood being flung from his nose. He worked shy of Gilmer for several steps as the pair continued to circle each other. Ship got Gilmer with a glancing blow from a solid fist and then lurched forward and wrapped both arms around Gilmer, lifting his opponent off the ground.

Gilmer got his hands above Ship's arms and jabbed both elbows into his opponent's chest.

"Now," Rollo shouted. "Crack a few ribs!!"

Gilmer leaned back from Ship's tightening grip and snapped his head forward into Ship's already injured nose. Ship didn't release Gilmer until the older man slapped his hands flat against each of Ship's ears at the same moment.

Ship dropped Gilmer and leaned down, reaching for his ears. Gilmer snapped his head into Ship's forehead, which laid the man out on his back — unmoving.

"I'd count that as an 'Uncle,'" Ethan said.

Rollo couldn't believe it. He looked down at his cousin in the dirt.

"Who's next?" Gilmer barked.

Ethan stepped forward with his palm up. "If you can't count your money, I'll do it for you."

Rollo sagged and handed Ethan a hand full of coins. Ethan turned to Tyner and asked, "What do you figure the damage is?"

CHAPTER 20

Bell rushed forward as Gilmer picked up his blade and pistol from off his hat in the dirt. She grabbed his arm and looked into his face.

"Uncle Gilmer, I was worried about you."

"No need, hon," he said, reaching for this hat. "I used to do this all day when I was a mountain man. Fights would last for an hour each sometimes. This was nothin'."

Ethan returned the rest of Rollo's money to him and said, "Now, leave. And when you come back, no guns."

Rollo helped the recovering Ship to his feet, as did the younger cousin El.

"Never seen Ship get beat b'fore. I can't even beat him." Then, looking at Ethan and Tyner, Rollo said, "We'll leave — and no guns when we come back. That was the bargain. Us McMulliens keep our word."

Back at Hedgecock's store, Gilmer and Ethan saw to the buying of several tents and tools. Odel was still outside with the wagons talking to a few blacks in the road.

After all the shopping was done and paid for, Abe Hedgecock told Gilmer, "It will take a while to load all this. So you folks might want to go get a bite to eat."

Vella and Bell thought this a good idea.

"Your pick of some tasty places to chow down is right up the street — both sides of the road. Pick any of them. You can't go wrong."

"Appreciated," Ethan said as the party headed for the boardwalk.

When they told Odel the plan, he bit his lip and looked down before he looked up and said, "If it's the same t' you," he to Ethan, "I think it might cause less trouble if I go somewhere else. I was told of a place by some people who passed by while I was out here."

"It's OK with me," Ethan said. "Don't rush yourself. We'll meet you back here when we're all done."

Odel nodded and left, headed across the road and around the nearest corner.

"Odel is trying to save us all from starting something," Gilmer said. "He'll feel better eating somewhere else."

The rest of the party understood. Blacks and whites lived separate lives since the war. It was a peaceful co-existence, but prejudice still ran deep in Texas and nationwide. Slavery was not something that was ended quickly. But afterward, life for all required accommodations to keep down smoldering rage among blacks and whites. As a mulatto, Odel found himself often straining to fit in.

Vella, Bell, Gilmer, and Ethan walked in the opposite direction and decided on a cafe to eat.

⁂

While they ate, Ethan told them what he's learned at the Land Office and showed them the map Littleton Tyner and drawn for him.

"I was thinking we could take a look at that sawmill first and then move back this way," he pointed toward Daingerfield, "to find us land."

"We can't make it all the way down there today," Gilmer said.

"No, I think we'll spend the night on the road. But it will give us a full day to examine that mill and go look for land. We'll have to depend on Odel for a decision about that mill."

Bell said, "Those McMulliens don't live down that way, do they?"

Ethan laughed. "No. They live somewhere north of town, the land agent said."

"Good."

"You still worried about me?" Gilmer asked.

"No — but — yes," the youngest member of their party said.

Gilmer laughed. "My sense is that those boys are too young to be so big and strong. They've got more muscles than brains — but I think they'll keep their word."

"The land agent says they are dirt poor but save every penny. They then can come to town every now and again to let loose. He says they're not bad people — just uneducated and, like he said, not grown up."

"We may want to hire them once we find us a place," Gilmer said.

"Hire them?" Bell gasped.

"There's going to be a lot of hard work ahead of us," Ethan chimed in. "If they're good workers, I'd give them a chance."

"Men," Vella said, shaking her head.

Ethan smiled and chuckled. "Don't you worry? Gilmer will keep them and anybody else we hire in line. But a strong back and a weak mind could be just the ticket for us."

They did stop and made camp a few hours later. Ethan and Gilmer pulled out one of the tents and put it up. It was 6 feet high and a dozen feet long.

"Ladies," Ethan announced when it was erected, "how'd you like a little more privacy for the night?

Vella and Bell exchanged books of delight. She looked at Ethan with sincere appreciation.

"Thank you. That is very thoughtful. Aren't you going to put one up for yourselves?"

"Outside is still good for us," Gilmer said. "We needed to see how to put up one of these things — but as long as we're still standing guard..."

"And it doesn't rain," Ethan cut in.

"Right," Gilmer went on. "We'll be all right."

Odell returned from hobbling the mules and Ethan's horse.

"What we need," Odel said, sitting down and beginning to eat his supper, "is a couple of dogs."

Gilmer looked up smiled. "Hunting dogs. Quail, dove, turkey, and ducks."

"We should be on the lookout for some."

"Puppies?" Bell asked.

"That would be best," Ethan said.

"We could train them — and they'd be natural watchdogs."

"I like dogs," Vella said.

"Not cats?" Ethan asked.

"I grew up around dogs," she said, remembering. "I think I've missed having some around."

"I'm sure we can fix that," Ethan said.

CHAPTER 21

The wagons reached the Rowling place by mid-morning the next day. The house was leaning and had watermarks two feet above the ground. When stopped, a young man appeared from the back of the house. He was skinny, had hollow cheeks, and was scruffy. His red-rimmed eyes and bare feet were the first things everyone noticed. He wore bibbed overalls with only one strap over his naked shoulders.

"Davis Rowling?" Ethan asked.

"Yep," the boy in his late teens said, his hands in his pockets.

"I'm Ethan Andrews. The land agent in Mt. Pleasant said you had a sawmill you wanted to sell."

"It's behind th' house — a little ways back."

"Can we take a look at it?"

"Sure. But it's been flooded. So if you buy it, you're goin' a' have t' move it somewhere else."

"Let's take a peek first," Ethan said.

Davis Rowling turned and waved for Ethan to follow. Ethen climbed down and handed the reins to his horse to Vella. Gilmer set his brake and followed Odel to the ground. The three men went around the house on foot and followed the young man.

The land around the house and approaching the mill was all clean cut. Even the stumps had been removed. The sawmill sat on a platform that appeared to have moved from its original location by several yards. Weeds were thick, and life was returning since the months following the flood.

"Here she is," Davis said, climbing up on the platform.

Signs of water up 3 feet and a little more were evident on the platform's weight-bearing posts and over the equipment. Odel checked the engine and the boiler. Gilmer looked around at the stand of tools. Ethan saw how the leather belts had dried and cracked.

After Odel had examined the whole platform, he stepped over to Ethan and Gilmer.

"The motor is all right. It was sealed. Even the boiler's all right. It needs a good cleaning and a new belt or two if we can't get these back in shape. The saw blades are a little rusted and would need sharpening — but I think it would all work."

"All right," Ethan said and turned to Davis. "What are you askin' for it?"

"I don't know," the boy said. "A hundred dollars?" Hell, for a hundred and fifty dollars, you can buy th' whole lot — house, land and all."

Gilmer and Odel had to look away to keep from revealing their shock and amazement.

"How much land is it?" Ethan asked.

"Sixty acres."

"Is it all like this?" Ethan gestured to the overgrown land they'd just walked.

"Most of it. There's still a section of uncut woods."

Ethan looked over at Gilmer and Odel, who had regained their composure. "I say, we buy it — all of it." Ethan turned to Davis and offered his hand, saying, "One hundred and fifty dollars."

"Cash on the barrel head, Davis said.

"Done. Meet me in two days at a bank in Mt. Pleasant."

"That'll be the Atlas Bank," Davis said.

"Atlas Bank," Ethan repeated.

"Aren't we cheating that boy?" Vella called to Ethan when they had the wagons headed east. He pulled over to the side of the road and waited for the first wagon to catch up with him.

Riding beside the wagon with Vella only a few feet away, Ethan said, "Let's see if the land is free and clear. Odel says the mill's going to need more than a little work to be ready to use. We'll have to move it — most likely take it apart and put it back together. But we won't do wrong by the boy. I'd hire him, but I have the sense he doesn't take to hard work."

He rode beside the wagon for a bit more and then said, "No matter what we pay him, I doubt there will be much of it left 6 months to a year from now."

Vella reluctantly nodded her head in agreement. "All we can do is be fair."

Ethan agreed and rode on ahead.

After they had been traveling for about an hour, Ethan pulled over once more, waiting for the second wagon this time.

"What do you think?" he asked Gilmer. "I like what I see."

"Enough woods to feed a sawmill for years," Gilmer concerned, giving a glance to Odel, who also agreed. "The ground looks like it would grow anything."

"What about cattle?"

"I get the feelin' this is not the best ranching country."

"Want to keep moving on west? Maybe south?"

Wilber mulled this over before he spoke. "I can't see us leavin' this fine land. If I have to, I'll find something else t' do. I know you don't herd dairy cows — but this seems like a place we could do well."

"That's my thinking, too," Ethan said. "There's a town ahead, called Daingerfield. What's say we stop there, get you a horse, and give this country a good look."

"I'm with you,' Gilmer said.

Ethan rode up beside Vella and Bell.

"We'll stop at a town called Daingerfield. Then Gilmer and I are going to ride some of it."

CHAPTER 22

Ethan led the Star AT group southeast down the road past the burned-out remains of the first town of Daingerfield. The year before, ablaze, all but erased the original town. Daingerfield had moved a half-mile. It was now beside the new Louisiana, Arkansas and Texas railroad tracks.

The first townsite was where a band of 100 men fought a bloody battle with Indians near a natural spring in 1830. Capt. London Daingerfield, the leader of the Texas forces, was killed, but a town began to grow up in the area. A decade later, it was named in his honor.

What greeted the AT was over a dozen new structures, with a few more still under construction. First, they passed a church/schoolhouse. Besides the usual mercantile and three saloons, there were two liveries, the first is Duff Sprague's — he's a blacksmith. The new town also had a post office, an eatery, a saddlery, a gunsmith, and a doctor's office. There was even an undertaker and empty local jail. The train depot with the freight office and telegram was at the far end of the main road, where the train tracks were. Beyond the tracks, sitting on a rise, was a stone-based school.

"That's the Sylvia Academy," a pale-skinned man of 30 said from the boardwalk. He wore a white apron with the top folded down and the rest tied around his waist. "It's a private school for girls."

The man on the porch of the mercantile was reading a two-page paper. He looked somehow familiar, but Ethan couldn't place him.

"Hedgecock?" Vella asked, looking up at the sign over the store.

"You been to Mt. Pleasent?" the man said with a smile.

Bell looked from the man to the sign and back again.

"You met my older brother, Abe. My son, Bluford, works for him. When he's ready — and Abe and I have the money — Bulford's going to open a new store — our biggest — west in Sulpher Springs. I'm Sanders Hedgecock," the pale-skinned man said.

"We're the Star AT. I'm Vella Andrews. That fellow on the horse over there is my husband, Ethan. This is his sister Bell beside me, Mr. Hedgecock."

"My pleasure, ladies," the man said, nodding his head. "Mr. Andrews."

"Our partner Gilmer is driving the second wagon," Vella went on. "Our friend Odel is with him."

"Andrews and Thebadeau — Star AT," the store owner said after a moment. "Passing through?"

"We'll see," Ethan said. "Could be we could be neighbors — and regular customers."

"Well, now. What can I do to help make that come true?"

"Tell me where I can rent a horse and a safe place to park the wagon for a few hours."

"Your wagons are safe anywhere. We have a jail but no lawman. Duff Sprague handles any trouble we have around here. So far, we don't need a real lawman. Could be because we don't have any lawyers either," he said with a laugh at his own joke. "You can get at horse at Vaughn Janney's livery," Sanders Hedgecock said, pointing at livery not far from the tracks.

"Obliged," Ethan said. Then, he turned to Gilmer, "Let's park the wagons and eat before you and I take a tour."

"Go down toward the depot," the mercantile owner said. "Turn to your left. There's some open lots there."

"I'll get you a horse and meet you all back at the cafe." Then Ethen had a thought and turned back to Hedgecock. "Will they give Odel any trouble if he eats with us?"

"Retta Lobdell is about as good a Christian woman as you'll ever find. Her doors are open to all."

Ethan tipped his hat and headed back up the street toward the livery as Vella and Gilmore started the wagons in the direction of the depot.

⁂

Gilmer's rented horse was a buckskin. The gelding quickly responded to Gilmer's commands with only the slightest action from him.

He and Ethan took the road toward Mt. Pleasant. They turned into wooded land after a mile. The land they found was a mix of forests, meadows, and clear running streams.

When they pulled to a stop to let their horses drink, "What do you think?"

"Sure as hell ain't cattle country. But it is great for everything else. I'm no farmer, but I can see raising horses, lumber — and cotton will be our best bet."

"Are you all right with that?"

"Oh, as long as I can make a living, I'm OK. Never done any farming — but I can learn."

"What would you say to marking our land this way. Say from the crossroads where the Daingerfield to Pittsburg road meets the Mt. Pleasant road?"

"Good for me. Would that run down to the Rowling land?"

"It will take a survey from the Land Agent to know. I'm thinking we should file on a thousand acres. This land is cheap, and it would give us a bigger chance of making it."

"Fine with me," Gilmer said. "You and Vella are keeping track of the books and the money, so if you two think it's a good idea, I'll go along."

CHAPTER 23

Back in Daingerfield, Ethan and Gilmer returned to their camp beside the wagons in the open lot. Ethan and Gilmer told of the land they had seen. Ethan said he thought they might want to get a thousand acres instead of 500.

Bell and Vella agreed.

"There are a few things we still need," Gilmer said. "A big roll of twine — for measuring — some water pumps. The springs running through the place are great, but we'll all get tired of carrying the water in buckets pretty quick. I know Bell has one in her wagon, but we're going to need more."

"And a keg or two of nails," Ethan added.

"How about a roll of wire?" Gilmer asked.

"So, back to Hedgecock's," Bell said.

"Shouldn't we start an account if we're going to be living near here?" Vella asked.

"Yes," Ethan agreed. "And Gilmer reminded me, we need to get an account book. You and I will be keeping up with our finances."

"All right," Vella said. She pulled a copy of a newspaper out of her pocket. "I thought you might want to see this."

The paper was "The Mount Pleasant Herald." It had been the same paper Sanders Hedgecock had been reading earlier in the day. The story Vella pointed out was the arrest of two bank robbers. According to the article, Cyrel Kitchens and Lamar Uhlrich were arrested for brawling in the French Quarter of New Orleans. The two intoxicated men identified themselves as members of the Slade Staker gang. The New Orleans Police Department knew the gang had been responsible for a double bank robbery and murder in Texarkana. The pair of outlaws were to be turned over to Texas Rangers for transport back to the twin cities. Ethan read out loud so Gilmer would know.

Ethan looked up, saying, "They don't say anything about Staker. I suspect he is still free and will leave the pair who were arrested to their own fate."

Gilmer said, "Think Staker is still looking for us for killin' his brother back in Arkadelphia."

"I wouldn't doubt it."

"Than we all need to stay on guard," Gilmer said.

"To that point," Bell said, "are we still interested in dogs? The lady that owns the cafe said the blacksmith has some he's been trying to give away. They're getting big, and he's tired of feeding them."

"What kind are they?" Ethan wanted to know.

"She didn't say."

"We want hunting dogs," Gilmer said.

"She did say they were still puppies but weaned." Then, Bell asked, "Can we take a look at them tomorrow?"

"Sure," Ethan said. "But you also ought to write your Uncle Bill again. Tell him where we are. He can write to us here, care of the Star AT."

"I'll take care of that first," she said.

Ethan looked up to the group and said, "I need to ride up to Mt. Pleasant and get the Land Agent and the bank to start getting the survey and the paperwork done on the land."

"Don't forget meeting Davis Rowling," Vella reminded him.

"Oh, that's right."

"Now we all have something to do tomorrow," Bell smiled.

Riding up the road to Mt. Pleasant, Ethan was approached by 2 horses carrying 3 scrawny, ragged teenage boys. It was near Swauano Creek. The better of the two horses, a red dun with its ribs showing, was double ridden by a pair of seeding and up kemp rascals. The other mount, a swayback piebald, was ridden by a skin-and-bones saddle tramp who wasn't old enough to grow a beard that was more than thin separated patches of light brown hair.

As they approached, the riders did not move to give way to Ethan. Instead, they stopped side by side, blocking the road. The double-ridden red dun's second rider pulled up a single barrel shotgun. The rider of the piebald pulled a rusted Colt single-action Army Revolver. Both weapons were aimed at Ethan.

"Hold up there, mister!" the leader, the skinniest with pale blue eyes on the swayback, said.

Ethan kept approaching until he was almost on top of the trio. He yanked back on his bridle and pulled to the left. His paint reared up and swung left, causing the two robbers' horses to buck and twist away — dumping all the riders. When the three young men regained their knees, they faced Ethan with both pistols as he sat in his saddle.

The would-be robbers raised their hands and got to their feet.

"Please, mister," the leader said. "We're just hungry. Ain't ate in two days."

"We did have some grass this morning," the first passenger of the red dun said. This one had bloodshot eyes.

"None of our guns are loaded," the one who had held the shotgun said. "If we did, we'd go hunting."

"We're s' hungry," their leader said sadly, "our stomach thinks our throats have been cut. So go ahead and shoot us. It'll put us out of our misery."

Ethan looked over the three and finally holstered his two revolvers.

"Are you boys afraid of work?"

"Look at us. Nobody wants to hire us. We'd do anything but folks just laugh at us."

It was a long minute before Ethan spoke.

"Get on your horses and keep going to Daingerfield. Go toward the tracks and the depot. Left of the last building, you'll find two wagons and a tent before you get to the tracks. Ask for Gilmer Thebadeau. Tell him I've just hired you."

"Hired — us?" the scrawny leader asked, looking at the other two and back at Ethan.

"The Star AT."

"Where's that?"

"You're going to help build it. Three meals a day and a place to sleep. If you work out, $30 a month."

The young men were stupified.

"Why would you do that?" their leader asked slowly.

"I either hire you — or shoot you. Which do you prefer?"

"Mr. Thebadeau," the shotgun holder said.

"Gilmer Thebadeau," said the young man who rode double in front of the one with the shotgun.

"You're jobs don't start for two days. So you'll have to get some kind of jobs around town for a meal each day — but come back to the wagons for supper. Can you do that?"

"Yes, sir," all three said quickly.

"There a creek nearby the wagons. A bath and clean clothes wouldn't hurt you get any job. Tell the local people you are asking for a job for a meal."

"And who are you," their leader asked.

"Ethan Andrews."

Nothing else was said by the three for a moment as they exchanged looks. Finally, their leader said, "I'm Homer Becorn. This is Jilson Elkins and Isom Ganninger. We'll prove ourselves, Mr. Andrews." Homer said. "And make the Star AT proud."

CHAPTER 24

The Atlas Bank in Mt. Pleasant looked like a stone fortress. However, with the bars on the windows and doors, it could also be a prison except for the castle look of the entire building.

"Sign here," Land Agent Littleton Tyner said, handing a fountain pen from his pocket to Davis Rowling. They were standing in the Atlas Bank president's office. Davis took the instrument and carefully wrote his name, which still looked like a child's idea of a cursive signature.

Tyner handed Ethan the clear land deed. After examining it, Ethan nodded to banker Bowman Poe, who counted out 400 dollars for the boy. The surprised young man had on boots and a faded shirt under his bib overalls, which he still wore with only one strap attached.

"Four hundred? I thought our deal was $150 — including the sawmill."

"It and the land is worth more, son," Ethan said. "I don't cheat people." Then, turning to the banker, Ethan asked, "Isn't that a fair price?"

"More than fair," the suited and glasses-wearing banker said. He was of average height and weight. His curly gray hair and neatly trimmed beard gave him the look of a lawyer or doctor. "Davis, you are fortunate to be dealing with honest people."

The boy nodded his head but said nothing as he looked at what seemed to be a small fortune.

"Don't waste it," Land Agent Tyner said. "Be careful, or you'll be dead broke and wishing you'd been smart about it."

"Thank you," Davis said, still looking at the money and addressing no one in particular.

Then Davis Rowling left the office, closing the door behind himself.

The three men watched the boy go before they turned back to the business at hand.

"Well," Tyner said, "since you're buying 1,000 acres, I decided a slight discount was in order. He showed the deed to Ethan and the banker. Poe picked up a mortgage document off his desk. All the information had been filled in — except for Tyner and Ethan's signatures.

"When Littleton attaches the survey to it, and both of you sign, we're in business." Bowman Poe said. "And with the down payment you've made, Atlas Bank is honored to have you as a customer."

Littleton Tyner picked up the deed.

"I'll be doing the survey myself. I have a man who helps me. When it's done, where can I find you, Ethan?"

"We're going to start in right away. So we'll be somewhere off the main road, cutting down trees and laying things out."

Bowman offered his hand to Ethan, who took it and shook it.

"We all expect the Star AT to be a welcome addition to this part of Texas," Tyner.

"That's our hope, too," Ethan said. "Now, where can I find The Mt. Pleasant Herold?"

Emit Voigtlander was the owner, reporter, editor, and typesetter of the weekly Mt. Pleasant Harold. He was a plump hairy man with ink-stained fingers and his glasses parked on the top of his balding head. In his middle 40s, he had seen enough life to jade anyone. Yet he had about him a glow of joy. He whistled as he worked.

When the front doorbell jingled, he looked up from his typesetting table to see Ethan enter.

"Be right with you," the man said and began humming as he finished setting the sentence he was working on. He wiped his hands on an already ink-stained rag as he crossed the room to Ethan.

"Ethan Andrews," he said, extending his hand.

"Emit Voigtlander," the editor said, accepting Ethan's hand.

"I'm looking for a ranch cook. Can you help me write a want ad?"

The journalist let laughter roll over him as he chuckled, "The Star AT, correct?"

"Yes. How did you guess?"

"The Star AT has a reputation. The McMulliens — Davis Rowling. Word gets around. Not newsworthy — yet — but I keep my ear to the ground and my finger to the wind." He laughed to himself. "I believe I can do better than help you write an ad." He stepped over to the front door, pulled it open, and called out, "Milburn Barcley! Go over to the Widow Pauley's. Ask her if she'd mind bringing my lunch to the office?"

"Sure thing, Mr. Voigtlander," came the voice of a boy out in the road.

"Have a seat," the editor said. "Can I offer you some coffee?"

"Yes," Ethan said, wondering what was going on.

"Tell me about the AT. I need a story for my next edition."

"Our story is just starting. We've not — ah —. We're still an idea. Littleton Tyner is going to do a survey, and we'll get started."

"But Bowman Poe is ready to give you a mortgage already."

"How did you know that?"

"Mt. Pleasant telegraph, of sorts — even gossip leads to news. And I keep my ear to the ground," Emit chuckled. "The front and back of two pages each week requires more words than you think."

"But your news isn't all local. I read about the bandits arrested in New Orleans. Where'd you get that story?"

"The New Orleans Picayune — Daily Picayune. Whew," Emit said wistfully, "daily. I should live so long." Then to Ethan, he said, "Newspapers share our material — as long as we give each other credit. Did you see 'The New Orleans Daily Picayune' at the top of the story you read?"

"Yes," Ethan said, "I guess I did."

"That's how I first heard about you."

"I don't understand."

"I read the story in The Arkansas Democrat. You killed one of the Staker brothers up in — Arkadelphia."

"We've been told he still wants to kill one of my partners and me."

The front doorbell tinkled.

Ethan looked up to see a woman of 30 with double dimpled cheeks, dressed in black and carrying a tin bucket.

The editor stood and said, "Widow Pauley. Thank you for doing this." He took the pail from her.

"Not at all," she said in a sweet voice.

"Mrs. Maude Pauley, meet Ethan Andrews."

Ethan was already on his feet and had removed his hat. "Mrs. Pauley."

She offered her hand, and as they shook, Emit took the pan out of the pail and set it on the desk. He put the fork beside it.

"This is for you," he said to Ethan.

"Huh?"

"Just sit down and eat."

"Please go ahead," Mrs. Pauley said.

Ethan sat and picked up the fork as the lady and the editor continued to talk.

"You wanted me to bring you your lunch — why?"

"What would you think about cooking for a farm/ranch crew?"

Maude Pauley was not expecting a question like that.

"Well — I don't see how that would differ from cooking for a boarding house."

Ethan was enjoying his first bite of stew and biscuits. Then, finally, he got up, wiping his mouth, and said, "Mrs. Pauley, we are building a horse ranch, a farm — with a sawmill — near Daingerfield -- and we need a cook. For a dozen or more when we get going."

"That's something I could do, Mr. Andrews — but I come with two children."

"A ranch is a great place to grow up. Especially, a building one."

Widow Pauley beamed at Ethan's response. "I've heard about your Star AT. I'd love to be your cook. How soon do you need me? I can't just get on a wagon and leave Mt. Pleasant."

"Of course not. Well, you need to order all the pots, pans, and whatever else you'd need. I'm sure you must already have some. My wife has already ordered a stove. I'll go set up an account at Hedgecock's. You go by and order whatever you need. By the way, did you know Mr. Hedgecock has a brother, and he runs the general store in Daingerfield?"

"No," she said. "That's convenient."

"Would it be possible for you to wrap up your affairs here in, say, a couple of weeks?"

"That would be plenty of time."

"I'll buy your house today," Emit Voigtlander. "You set the price, and I'll meet it."

Ethan said, "You won't be able to do much until the stove arrives — so ask Mr. Hedgecock how long it will take to have it get to you — at the depot in Daingerfield."

"You've got yourself a cook, Mr. Andrews."

They shook hands on the deal.

"Please make it, Ethan."

"And I'm Maude."

She turned to the editor and said, "Bless you, Mr. Emit Voigtlander."

"I promised Nicolas before he died that I'd look out for you and your children."

"It seems you have," she smiled. "But you're going to have to look for another place to live, Emit."

"Not if you sell to me. I'll just need to get a new cook — and housekeeper — and I'll take a bigger room for myself," the newspaperman said. Then, turning to Ethan, he said, "We both know her house was a little too small for boarders."

"You never complained, Emit," the lady said with a smile.

"What was there to complain about? I'm just saying the AT will suit you all much better."

"So do I," she said, dabbing a tear from her eye.

CHAPTER 25

Ethan returned to Daingerfield the next morning.

"I'm surprised to see you," Vella said when he looked up to see him leading his horse, plus 4 more saddled mounts up to their wagons. He got down and hitched the animals to the wagon.

"I expected some kind of hitch between the Land Agent and the bank — but it all worked out," Ethan said, getting down and looping all the reins over a wagon wheel. "And, I paid Davis Rowling $400 cash."

Vella smiled at that. "I shouldn't have doubted you."

"Have our new hires been behaving themselves?"

"All three of them. We're going to have to put some meat on those boys, Ethan. The first strong wind — and they're gone."

He laughed at the idea.

"They keep us well stocked with firewood," I'll say that for them. They're out finding something to do — but they'll be here promptly at supper time. You can bet on that."

Vella poured him a cup of coffee from the pot hanging over the fire.

Gilmer arrived with Bell. Each had a growing puppy attached to a piece of rope around a collar. They looked to be ready to move on from being puppies to dogs. They had a lot of learning to do, but both looked eager and came sniffing up to Ethan, who knelt and petted each in turn.

"They're part retriever and part pointer," Gilmer explained. "They'll hunt and be great watchdogs, too."

The two puppies all but knocked Ethan over, licking and nuzzling him in their enthusiasm. He only spilled some of his coffee.

"Brownie — Spot!" Bell laughed as he tried to corral both dogs off of Ethan.

Vella couldn't help but laugh. "They've certainly got the energy."

"Agreed," he said. "Where's Odel?"

They all looked about.

"He's here somewhere," Vella said.

"Here I am," Odel came around the wagon with a file in his hand. "I thought I'd make sure all the tools had a good edge on them for when we need them."

"I thought it might be a good day to do some other things. So I rented us some horses. Odel, I thought you could go down and check our sawmill — figure out how we're going to take it apart so we can move it." Ethan handed a bridle to one of the horses to Odel. "And look for a suitable spot to put it. I'll make sure it's inside our property line."

To Gilmer, he said, "We're going to need some hands, Gilmer — to move the mill and to start building things. I was wondering what your thoughts are about the McMulliens?"

"Strong backs and weak minds is what I think. Just what we'll be needing."

"I thought you might go see about getting them to work with us."

Gilmer took a bridle from the wagon wheel. "They'll sure be a help. But even with them — and the other three you hired, we'll need a couple more."

"Hire whoever you like. Then, come tomorrow, we can start to work."

"Where are you headed?" Gilmer asked.

"I thought I'd take the ladies out to pick out a spot for a homestead and cookshack."

"Why a cookshack first?" Vella asked.

"I hired us a cook — a widow — Mrs. Maude Pauley, who happens to have two children. I thought a cookshack with a long table and some benches would be a good idea with all of us -- including the new hands. We can all sleep in tents for a while longer if you ladies don't mind."

Vella and Bell exchanged glances.

"I can't argue with that," she said. "But it means we'll be cooking over an open fire for a while longer. Until my stove arrives."

"We'll set it up on some rocks under a tarp by the wagons as soon as it gets here. I told Mrs. Pauley you had ordered a stove. We can use the cookshack. If you'd rather, we can order a different stove for her. That way, you can still keep yours when we have a place to move in to."

"One stove will be fine. But, if she's going to be the cook — and I presume she's good ..."

"She is. I sampled her food."

"... then I'll wait and see. If I want a stove of my own, we can always order another."

"I will leave that up to you," Ethan said. "And if we're going to be out for the afternoon, I say we eat at the cafe tonight — including the new hands."

"I will go for that," Vella said, taking a set of reins.

"Do we just tie up the dogs here?" Bell wanted to know.

"For the moment. We won't forget about them."

❦

Gilmer thought to himself as he looked at the dirt and mud shack the McMulliens lived in, "This is got to be what they mean by dirt poor."

"Hello, McMulliens!" Gilmer called.

Two of the bib overall, stained long-sleeved undershirts and boots wearing hulks, came out the door and a third from the nearby corral.

"Why it's your friend," the older Rollo said, slapping' Ship on the back. Then, to Gilmer, he said, "Come back for a rematch?"

"Does he need one?"

Rollo got a belly laugh out of that.

Ship rolled his shoulders and flexed his arms.

"I came," Gilmer said, "to see if you boys wanted a job."

"What kind of job?" the younger one, El, asked.

"Does it much matter?" Gilmer responded. "There's $30 a month and food if you can stick with it."

"A steady job?" Rollo asked. "For how long?"

"As long as you're man enough to do it — and behave yourselves."

The three cousins looked at each other a little suspiciously.

"Why us?" Ship asked, stepping forward."

"We're building a place from scratch. First thing is we'll be moving a sawmill and getting it up and running. Then we're building a farm and horse ranch. After that, fences to be built, buildings to be put up, and a lot of trees to be cut. It's work, but it's steady — so is the food."

El said to Rollo and Ship, "We never had a steady job."

"Cause nobody wanted to keep us around," Rollo said.

"You'll be required to bathe regular — you'll be working and living with others."

There was nothing more said by anyone for several moments.

"Well," Gilmer finally broke the silence, "are you interested or not?"

"We're thinkin' it over," Rollo said. "What about our place here?"

"It's still yours. On your days off, if you want to come work on it, that's up to you."

"What is this place you're talkin' about, and where is it?"

"It's the Star AT — close to Daingerfield."

Again, the trio looked from one to the other.

"We'll give it a try," Rollo finally said. "When do we go to work?"

"As soon as you get there." Gilmer sat his horse a moment longer. "Jest so I'm sure — your names are Rollo, Ship — and El?

"You got it right," Rollo said. When Gilmer didn't turn to go, " Rollo asked, "There somethin' else?

"It's only fair t' tell you — there's an outlaw — Slade Staker. He might come lookin' t' kill us — me and Ethan — Ethan Andrews. He's my partner."

The McMulliens looked at each other. Rollo said, "Sounds like we'd better take our guns."

CHAPTER 26

"Some church ladies made us a potluck lunch for painting the church." Homer Becorn was talking while his companions, Jilson Elkins and Isom Ganninger, ate in the cafe in Daingerfield.

"Church ladies are great cooks," Isom said. He was one of the trio who tried to stop Ethan on the Mt. Pleasant road.

"We need to remember that," Jilson Elkins said. "Maybe we should think about going to church. Regularly, I mean."

"I think our cleaning up also helped," Homer said, reaching for another biscuit to sop up his gravy.

The whole AT crew was eating at the Daingerfield cafe labeled "Eats." The three newest and youngest members of the AT sat at one table with Odel, who ate without talking. Ethan, Vella, Bell, and Gilmer were enjoying their meal of steaks, potatoes, biscuits, and gravy at a nearby table.

"What about the McMulliens?" Ethan asked Gilmer. "You hire them?"

"I did. But I told them they'd have to measure up. Said we'd give them a try."

"And," Vella said to Gilmer, "what do we know about them?"

"They have a place of their own — of sorts," Gilmer said. "They live in a dirt shack. From what I can tell, they're not much as farmers."

"But you think they'll work out for us?" she wanted to know

"We'll have t' see."

Ethan turned to Bell, "How are our watchdogs?"

Bell looked up from Brownie and Spot. "Uh — they're growing."

Ethan, Vella, and Gilmer laughed.

Ethan leaned back and called over to the other table.

"Isom, you any good with that .410 of yours?"

"Fair," the sharp cheekbones, narrow-lipped lad shrugged.

"Fair?" Jilson Elkins said. "He's been the one who's fed us mostly since they made us leave th' orphanage. Squirrels, rabbits, quail, doves — even a turkey one time."

"Then," Ethan said, "we need to get you some shells. You can go hunting with Gilmer. He's got a .12 gage in his wagon and a couple of boxes of birdshot."

"You can help me train th' dogs," Gilmer added.

"I'd like that," the boy said.

"Homer, how about that pistol of yours?" Ethan asked the leader of the three boys. "Can you hit the side of a barn with it?"

The teen with pale blue eyes had given up on trying to grow a beard and had shaved off the patches of brown hair on his sinewy cheeks. He snickered, "Ain't never tried. I found that ol' thing in the barn a week 'fore I run away from home. It's a cap and ball gun. I never fired it."

"Why'd you run away from home?" Bell asked.

"I was number 6 in the family — the runt of the litter. All my brothers kept whoopin' on me. I finally had enough of it. I took Nelly, that ol' swayback, and left. If I hadn't met up with Jilson and Isom, I would have starved t' death fer sure."

"Save up your money and bring it to the gunsmith here. See if he can convert it or if he'll let you trade it in on something better."

"Boys, are you ready to go to work tomorrow?" Ethan asked.

"Yes," Homer said. "But we don't always know what to do. My daddy was a mighty poor farmer. These two grew up in an orphanage."

"If you ever have a question, see somebody at this table," Ethan said, "or Odel. He knows there's always something that needs to be done."

Vella spoke to Odel. "Did you get everything you needed?"

"Yes, ma'am."

She turned to Ethan and told him, "Odel needed beeswax and a stiff brush for the belts of the sawmill. So I put them on our account at Hedgecock's. I also told Sanders always to allow Odel to get anything he needed."

"Good," Ethan said.

"What's the plan for tomorrow?" Bell asked, slipping a bit to the puppies under the table.

"Vella, Bell, and I found a place to build. We'll need to cut a road to the site so the wagons can get there. Then we need to set up tents down below by a creek. I expect we will be there for a while." Ethan leaned back and called over to Odel, "Are we ready to start breaking down and moving the sawmill?"

Odel said, "Yes, sir."

"What are we going to build first?" Vella asked.

"The cookshack and the bunkhouse."

Vella smiled. "Taking care of our people before ourselves. I like that, Ethan."

"I wanted to make sure it was OK with you first — but that was my plan."

"Whatever you think is best."

CHAPTER 27

A rough trail was cut through the trees to the homestead. The wagons were parked nearby — down by a stream. The boys helped clear the trail making it into a proper ranch road. It was to become their outlet to the Mt. Pleasant to Daingerfield road. They planted a sign with the Star AT brand burned in on the road to announce their presence.

A total of 3 tents were erected. One for Vella and Bell, one for Gilmer and Ethan, and the largest for Odel, Homer, Isom, and Jilson. The homesite was on a plot, which was a raised plateau with some large trees on it. The tents were below near the wagons.

Together, Ethan and Gilmore staked out where the dog-run house would be — facing the path out to the main road. They also marked where the cookshack and bunkhouse would be. Two decent-sized rooms were to be attached to the kitchen for Mrs. Maude Pauley and her children.

Midday on the second day, the three McMulliens arrived. They led a packhorse with gear they couldn't carry on their backs. Gilmer put Rollo and Ship to digging post holes for the corral. El and Ethan collected a toolbox from the Studebaker wagon and rode out to locate the sawmill.

Along the way, Ethan asked, "El. What kind of name is that?"

"A shortened one. El for Elwood. Rollo is Rolando, and Ship is Shipman."

"Interesting. Well, if it works for you, it's okay with me."

Ethan and El tied up their horses and loosened their cinches before stepping up on the platform where all the machinery was located.

They found Odel was busy rubbing beeswax into 3-inch wide leather belts. All the straps had been unstrung from pullies and been removed. He had a damp rag, a bucket of water, and a stiff wire brush on the floor beside the bench on which he sat.

"What can we disassemble?" Ethan asked.

Without pausing his work on the leather, Odel said, "I've drained the water from the boiler. After disconnecting the steam pipe at the top, you can then loosen all the bolts at the bottom of the boiler to its holding plate. There are also bolts from the holding plate to the floor."

Ethan turned to El, "Can you climb up on top of the boiler and work on that connecting? I'll get the big wrench."

The youngest McMulliens frowned a moment, then shrugged and climbed up on the metal box. He was straddling the curved top of the boiler when Ethan handed him the largest wrench. It took several tries before the nut began to budge.

Ethan and El spent their time freeing the metal box from its holding plate and then the plate from the floor. All the time, Odel continued to work on belts.

A triangle Ethan didn't remember buying rang in the distance when the sun was at its peak.

"Lunch must be ready," Ethan said, looking up from the floor. He got to his feet, and El followed.

As the two men stepped down to their grazing horses, Ethan called back to Odel, "You coming?"

"As soon as I finish this belt. 'Can't leave it half done."

Ethan and El tightened their cinches and got in the saddle.

As they loped toward the main camp, El said, "I don't want to cause problems, Captain."

"I was never in the Army, El."

"Sorry — boss. It's jest — I never took orders from a nigger b'fore."

"You know how to run a steam engine and a sawmill?"

"No, sir."

"Neither do I. Odel does. Who do you figure ought to be in charge of this job?"

"Yes, sir," El said, understanding.

"Also, remember this. As Gilmer says, 'When did you pick your parents?'"

"Pick?"

"You are who you are because of who they were." Ethan let that idea stew for a moment. "You had no choice in the matter." Then Ethan added, "The same is true for Odel. Maybe you can explain that to your cousins."

※

Where's Odel?" Vella asked when Ethan and El arrived.

"He's finishing up something he's working on. He should be along in a minute."

"We weren't sure you heard me," Vella indicated the metal triangle hanging from a nearby tree.

"We heard it — eventually. At first, I wasn't sure what it was. I didn't know we had a dinner chime."

"Picked it up in Mt. Pleasant. Come sit down and eat while it's hot."

Odel arrived a minute later. He loosened his cinch, and the mule he was riding started munched on the grass. He petted Brownie and Spot, who were jumping around.

Looking up at the homestead site, Ethan saw a few fence posts tilting as they sat in the empty holes.

"Looks like you made some progress," Ethan said the Gilmer.

"Most of th' holes are dug," Gilmer said, looking up from the tin pan in his lap. "Rollo and Ship are gophers with them posthole diggers."

"I hope you are using gloves," Vella said to the McMullens.

"Don't need 'em," Rollo said. "We're used to blisters."

"We have to work for these callouses," Ship said, holding up one red and tough hand.

"I've got the younger boys," Gilmer said, pointing to Homer, Jilson, and Isom, "collecting and shaping up some of the small trees they cut for the road into fence posts."

"We *are* using gloves," Homer said.

"But them and this food make it all worth it," the usually quiet Jilson said.

"Amen," Ship agreed. "We've never eaten this well in our whole lives."

"We're trying to do our part," Bell said, hugging Vella's arm.

"Keep up the good work," Ethan said. "You two are what's keeping all of us going."

"We could have them posts all in before we finish this evening," Gilmer said. "How are you two doing?" he asked Ethan and El.

"Slowly but surely. Most of the bolts are all but rusted in place. And we've just tackled the boiler. We have the engine, the flywheel, and all the carriage to go."

"I've been thinking about moving all this," Odel said. "I think we're going to need to build some skids and maybe even use all four mules in harness to get it done."

"I can believe that," Ethan said. "That boiler is solid steel. So is the flat plate it sits on."

"Don't we need to build the shed for all that before we move anything?" Gilmer asked.

"Absolutely," Ethan said. "I think we're talking about cutting some of the bigger trees and splitting them for a floor."

"Isn't that what we're going to need for the cookshack and bunkhouse?" Vella asked.

"Yes," Ethan said.

"I saw some big logs at the edge of the creek," Bell said.

"We'll need to move those to the pond beside the new mill site," Odel said.

"Move them? Why?"

"Wet wood cuts better than dry wood," Odel explained. "That's why the place we're shifting the mill to is beside a pond. We'll need to put all the logs we intend to cut in there — get them soaked for a couple of weeks when we can."

"I never knew that," Ethan admitted.

Vella was the one who spotted the rider approaching down their newly cut road, leading a packhorse with a light load.

CHAPTER 28

Land Agent Littleton Tyner was the rider who led a packhorse down from the ranch road to the wagons and tents. The clean-shaven, barrel-chested land agent wasn't wearing the sleeve garters Ethan had come to associate with him. Still, he did wear a starched collared white shirt.

Ethan met him, saying, "Step down, Mr. Tyner. We're finishing lunch. Can we offer you a plate?"

Ethan glanced at Vella.

"There is plenty," she said.

"That would be much appreciated," Tyner said, getting down and removing his hat. He had to wipe his prominent forehead and ran a bandana over his thinning blonde hair.

"Mr. Tyner is the Land Agent who directed us to this place," Ethan said to everyone. Then he introduced Vella, Bell, and Gilmer as his partners and pointed out the rest as the AT's crew.

"I'm pleased to meet you all. I see," Tyner said, looking up at the posts already set in the ground above on the homestead plot, "you've been very busy."

"No grass is growing under these boys," Gilmer said.

Homer had finished eating and slipped his pan into the larger bucket for dirty dishes. "Let me take your horses to water, sir," he said.

"Thank you very much," Tyner said, handing his reins to the thin young man. To Ethan, he said, "The fellow I usually work with surveying is off working for someone else today. I was hoping you might want to give me a hand and walk your land yourself, Ethan."

Ethan looked over at Odel. "Do you need a third set of hands to free the rest of the machinery?"

"I don't think so," he said. "El and I should be able to handle it."

Ethan glanced at El, who seemed to accept the idea. "Then I think I can."

Before he sat down, the land agent said to Ethan, "Emit Voigtlander told me to tell you that Slade Staker and two other bandits were arrested trying to rob a bank in Beaumont. The story will be out in Saturday's paper, but Emit said you might want to know right away."

"We do," Ethan said. "I killed his brother," Ethan paused as if remembering the moment and sighed. Then, when he continued, he said, "The two of them — brothers — tried to shoot Gilmer when we were in Arkadelphia, Arkansas. We found a youngster shadowing us after we left Texarkana. He said Staker wants to kill us. So it's good news to know he's been arrested."

"Emit said the three of them will stand trial and most likely end up in prison at Huntsville."

"We can hope," Vella said, handing Littleton a plate of food.

"Thank you, ma'am. This looks delicious."

After eating, Littleton Tyner and Ethan left to start their survey at the road intersection between Mt. Pleasant and Daingerfield Road and the one running from Daingerfield to Pittsburg. Tyner set up his tripod-mounted his transit atop it. He checked his compass and hung the plumb line from the tripod's center. It was then that he made his first mark on the survey plot he'd prepared in Mt. Pleasant. Ethan took the marker pole and the attached surveyor's chain as he and Littleton began pacing. One hundred links equaled feet. Eighty chains made up one mile. Ten square chains made one acre.

Back at the transit, the land agent used hand signals to move Ethan left or right until he was at the exact point. A marker was placed and the process repeated until all the land was marked. The job lasted the rest of the day. It was twilight before they returned to the AT camp.

***

Littleton entered the notes he had made all day into the survey back at the wagons as dinner was being served. Vella spooned up a pan of steak and potato for him. Before he accepted the meal, the land agent attached the survey sheet to the mortgage and signed off on the document.

Being early summer, the sun was still up as all the AT ate.

"You're going back to Mt. Pleasant this evening, Mr. Tyner?" Bell asked.

"Yes. I will sleep in my bed tonight."

"I offered him some space in a tent or some blankets on the ground," Ethan said.

"I'd rather ride a couple of hours, thank you very much," Tyner chuckled.

"You're welcome to stay," Vella offered.

"I appreciate the offer, but if I go after we eat, I can get the mortgage to the bank first thing in the morning."

"Perhaps after we get the operation going," Vella said. "You're always welcome."

"Certainly. If the food is as good as it is now, I will be looking forward to it."

"Thank you," Vella said.

"We aim to have a roof over everyone's head before winter," Gilmer said.

Ethan said, "But I think I may have overestimated how quickly we could get the sawmill working. So, we need to buy some lumber. Then we all can work on cutting trees, digging wells, and building. We can move the mill later and get it working then."

"Let me recommend Hinyard's Lumber," Littleton Tyner said. "Alby Hinyard will treat you right."

"Alby Hinyard. I'll take a wagon up and find his mill tomorrow."

They finished eating, and Tyner motioned Ethan to a barrel top where the land agent spread out the mortgage document.

"All the partners need to sign this," Ethan said after he signed and offered Tyner's fountain pen to Gilmer and then Bell. Then, after Bell had signed, Ethan offered the pen to Vella.

"Me?" she asked.

"You're a partner, Vella — not just for the money you contributed — but for everything you've done. The AT wouldn't be what it is — and what it will be — without you."

This brought tears to Vella's eyes as she took the pen and signed. And the name she signed was Vella Andrews.

CHAPTER 29

The land agent was in the saddle and gone before it was dark. Gilmer returned from spending a half-hour training Brownie and Spot. The partners drank coffee around the remainder of the fire Vella and Bell had used to cook supper over. Even Bell was learning to drink the stable drink of the nation.

"How are the McMullens working out?" Ethan asked.

"Fine," Gilmer responded. "They're not lazy. Fact is, they're hard workers all the way around."

"How about the younger three?"

"I think as long as we feed them, they'll never leave. Of course, they're not as strong as the McMullens — but you put them to a task, and they don't stop until it's done."

The group enjoyed a soft night as a full moon rose over the horizon.

"You know they call this a Comanche Moon," Gilmer said.

"Why?" Bell asked.

"They use the full moons to attack at night."

"Some stories I've heard about Comanche raids are nothing short of horrible," Vella said.

The conversation stopped when both dogs started barking. The sound of a galloping horse was heard coming down the newly cut road. A boy of about 8 rode a dapple-gray down by the wagons. Gilmer was up and grabbed the animal as the animal stopped.

"Whoa, there, girl! Hold up!"

The boy flung himself out of his saddle and spoke to Gilmer in a rush.

"Mr. Andrews," he asked, almost frantic.

"That's him over there," Gilmer said, gesturing with a thumb to Ethan, who had stood alone with Vella and Bell.

The boy flew to Ethan.

"Mr. Andrews, I'm Casper Sprague! My pa's Duff Sprague — the blacksmith! He was hit in the head by some railroad men in the Big Bull! They hit him with a full mug of beer and almost killed him! Mr. Hedgecock told me to come see if I could find you — and asked for your help!"

Ethan turned to Vella and asked, "Would you get my guns while I saddle up?"

She nodded and headed for the back of the wagon. Gilmer handed the reins of the boy's horse to Bell. "Walk him around a minute before you take him to the creek to drink."

"I'm going back with Mr. Andrews!" Casper Sprague said, still wound up.

"Let's make sure you don't kill your horse," Gilmer said as Bell was walking the sweat-drenched horse.

When Ethan came back down to the wagons, Vella had his gun belt ready for him. As he slipped it around his hips, the boy said, "I've got to get my horse!"

"Ride with me," Ethan said. The boy who had started toward the creek stopped in his tracks. He turned back to the wagons. Ethan extended a hand to Casper, and the boy swung up behind the saddle.

Ethan left at a lope and took the path up to the ranch road. Gilmer was not far behind as they both broke into a gallop once on the road proper.

Ethan and Gilmer thundered into town under the full glow of the Commanche Moon. The pale-skinned man with brown curly hair wearing a white apron, Sanders Hedgecock, stepped out into the street as Ethan and Gilmer pulled to a stop.

"Thank God you came," Sanders said.

"What's the problem?" Ethan asked.

"Four railroad men down at the Big Bull." The general store owner pointed at the saloon halfway down the street. "They're a track maintenance team — but they're mean drunks."

Casper Sprague slid to the ground. "Where's my pa?"

"Down in Doc Manheim's office."

The child ran off down the street.

"Are they armed?" Ethan asked as he stepped down and handed his bridle to Sanders Hedgecock.

"No. But a couple of them are big, and they're all drunk out of their minds."

"How many are they?" Gilmer asked, joining Ethan.

"Four. I've tried to keep an eye on them. The biggest one tried to go upstairs with one of the girls, but he couldn't make it. He's sitting on the steps. Two are at the bar, and one's at a table sitting in a chair."

Ethan nodded and glanced at Gilmer, who had his trapdoor Sharps in his hands. They headed toward the saloon.

Ethan and Gilmer looked in the saloon through the batwing doors. When they had the lay of the place, Ethan stepped in and kicked the legs of the chair, holding one of the railroad men who was leaning back. The man crashed to the floor on his back. Then, without slowing down, Ethan approached the drunkard, laughing at the bar. The butt of Ethan's revolver came down the man's back at the base of his neck. The man dropped like a 50-pound bag of flour.

The third man at the bar, mustached with dripping ends, was

holding one of the saloon girls tightly around the waist and was cutting off the front buttons of her tightly fitted corset. The moment his male companion dropped to the floor, the third man released the girl and flashed his knife out, ready to fight.

Ethan swung his model 3 Smith and Wesson. The barrel slammed into the man's forearm. The bone broke with a crack. The man dropped to his knees, holding his arm and screaming in pain.

Across the room, the railroad man who Ethan had dumped out of his chair shook his head. He reached for his pistol also on the floor only to have Gilmer stomp on his fingers. The man yelled, and Gilmer butt stroked him into the face — and the man slipped into the deep black.

The man with the broken arm looked up at Ethan, who, at that very moment, jammed an iron fist into the side of his head. This man joined his colleagues in the land of the unconsciousness.

The biggest of the lot, a man in striped bib overalls, heaved himself up from his slumping position and tried to stagger towards Ethan. But before he could take more than two strides, Gilmer was there in front of him, cocking his trapdoor Sharps. The man jerked to a stop recognizing the threat of the rifle.

"Going somewhere?" Gilmer asked.

"Uh — no, I don't think so," the man muttered.

Sanders Hedgecock opened the batwing doors and took in the scene in the bar.

Ethan called to him, "You got the keys to that new jail across the street?"

"Yes, sir, I do," Sanders said, reaching into his pocket to a metal ring of keys.

"Open up, and let's get these fellows into cells."

Gilmer, who had the full attention of the bulky man at the bottom of the stairs, said, "They're your friends! Pick 'em up!"

The still drunk man staggered forward but had enough strength to pick up both of his co-workers at the bar. He slung them over his shoulders. Ethan pointed toward the door with his pistol still in his hand.

The big drunken lug staggered out the door carrying his companions while Ethan and Gilmer grabbed the third by the back of his collar and dragged him outside, too.

CHAPTER 30

Doctor Rice Manheim, 33, a blonde, spare, with narrow shoulders, was a young man who wore spectacles. He had an air of quiet confidence about him as he came into the jail. Back in the cells, he splinted and wrapped the broken arm. When he returned to the office, Sanders Hedgecock locked the barred door.

Ethan and Gilmer waited in the jail's front room. When the physician returned, the doctor said, "That arm will heal in about 6 weeks if it's taken care of. I left his arm in a sling."

"How about the rest?" Ethan asked, parked on the sheriff's desk.

"A couple of broken teeth, big bumps, and bruises — plus the big one who's massively hungover. They'll all live — but they'll remember this night in Daingerfield."

From a chair by the lone table, Gilmer said, "Somebody should tell them to never come into town again — even if they're working the track that passes through."

"That would be the job of a sheriff or town marshal," the storekeeper said. "We don't have either. I think I told you, Duff Sprague usually took care of those kinds of things. He's a big man most folks don't want to cross."

"But they bashed him in the head with a mug of beer?" Ethan asked.

"That's what it looks like," the doctor said, closing up his bag on the table.

"Will he live?" Ethan asked.

"Oh, yes," Doc Manheim said. "He's got a concussion — his brain's been battered up to the top of his head. But he'll live. And if he follows my instructions, takes it easy for a week or so, he'll be as good as new. I expect Mrs. Sprague and their son Casper will see to that."

Ethan said, "Seem to me like you ought to pay your blacksmith what he's worth to be your part-time town marshal. After that run-in, he deserves it."

"Agreed," Sanders Hedgecock said. "This was more than we ever expected. But we're a growin' town. We need some kind of law. Thank you, gentlemen, for coming so quickly."

"Glad we could help," Ethan said, getting to his feet. "Doctor —"

"Manheim," the physician said. "Rice Manheim."

"Ethan Andrews," Ethan said, shaking hands with the doctor.

"Gilmer Thebadeau," his partner said, also taking the doctor's hand.

"Pleased to meet both of you," Doc Manheim said.

"We'll send the boy's horseback," Gilmer said, "when we can free up someone."

"No rush," Sanders said. "They have other horses in their corral. So it might be a few days before the boy is liable to need it again."

"If there's nothing else," Ethan said, "we'll be getting on back. We have a place to build."

"Daingerfield owes you both," Hedgecock said.

"Jest bein' a good neighbor," Gilmer said.

They tipped their hats and headed back to the AT.

Vella took Ethan in her arms and Bell hugged him from the side. The younger woman rushed over to Gilmer when he got down.

"We were worried," Bell said.

Vella didn't release Ethan but placed her head on his chest, and he felt the dampness of her tears on his shirt.

Ethan finally put his arms around Vella and rocked her until her breathing was back to normal.

Odel was up and took both horses to the newly build corral without a word.

When Vella was relaxed, she pulled away but didn't let go of Ethan's arms. "I've seen how quickly men can die."

Ethan said, "Gilmer and I know how to take care of ourselves."

"We know that," Bell said, still holding on to Gilmer's sleeve.

"But we couldn't help but worry," Vella said. "That's a woman's job, I suppose."

"We'll try not to put you in that position, any more than we have to," Ethan said.

"Are you hungry?" Vella said, wiping her cheeks on her sleeve. "It's so late that's there's not going to be much sleep tonight."

"I can alway eat," Gilmer said with a chuckle.

"Some coffee would be good," Ethan said, and the four of them headed down to the fire.

※

After his second cup of coffee, Ethan stood and said, "I think I'll take a walk."

"Would you mind some company?" Vella asked.

"I'd welcome it," he said, putting the cup down.

The pair walked up to the ranch road and stood as Ethan looked down the path in the remainder of the night's moonlight.

"What happened in town?" she asked.

Ethan described the events to her, but there seemed to be more when he finished. He and Vella stood in silence for a few minutes before Ethan began once more.

"I suspect Bell has told you I'm not her brother."

"She mentioned it. But I've never seen you be anything else to her but a protecting brother. She says you never talk about yourself or where you're from."

It took a couple of more moments before Ethan said, "I murdered a man in Missouri."

Vella had looped one of her arms in one of Ethans. She stepped away a half step but didn't let go of his arm as she examined his face.

"He must have deserved it," she said.

"He had raped my 16-year-old sister and was trying to steal a farmer's horse when my brother and I caught up with him."

"Then it would seem he needed to be killed."

"I didn't give him a chance. I had my pistol in his chest — and he decided to draw."

"Did he give your sister a chance?"

Ethan slowly shook his head.

"Seems to me he was asking to be killed," Vella said.

"I was going to kill him no matter what. Not for the horse he was trying to steal — but — for my sister. I know it didn't help her — but …?"

"He'll never do that to anyone else," Vella ended the thought for him.

"Any way you cut it, I still murdered him. He didn't have a chance."

"He didn't need a chance, Ethan. He didn't deserve to live with decent people after what he'd done."

"Was that my decision to make?"

"Who else would?"

"I didn't want my brother to have to live with it — so I did it."

"And you've been thinking you're a murderer ever since?" She looked him in the face with the moonlight making his eyes clearly visible. "Killing that Staker brother back in the Broken Wheel is haunting you, too, isn't it?"

"Did I have to actually kill him?"

"Both Stakers were trying to kill Gilmer. What else could you do?"

Ethan said nothing but did nod his head slightly.

"I was afraid I was going to have to kill someone tonight when they called us to town."

"I'm not the one to forgive you, Ethan — although I would," Vella said after a moment. "The man I've come to know in you is no killer. You do what has to be done — like you did tonight. Someone was in trouble, and you didn't hesitate. You raced off to help. That's not what a killer does."

Ethan took Vella in his arms and kissed her for the first time. It was a deep kiss full of longing and need but also a kiss of gentleness and understanding.

When they had both caught their breath, he said, "Ethan Andrews is not my real name. Gilmer doesn't even know that."

"It's the name that fits you — and it's a name fit for your new life. And for your new wife. So, I'm Mrs. Ethan Andrews and proud to be so."

He pulled her to him once more, and they kissed as the sun began to rise.

"Let's build the AT to be fit for us and our new life," she said.

CHAPTER 31

Over breakfast, Ethan and Gilmer decided to make a change. "Let's let the sawmill wait and turn the group's efforts toward cutting trees. Large and small -- where the house, cookshack, and dining hall, as well as the bunkhouse, will to be.

Ethan said to Homer Becorn, "How about you pick out a horse and lead the boy's horseback to Daingerfield."

"Yes, sir," Homer said.

Ethan and Vella exchanged glances occasionally but made it a point not to do so without the others being aware. There was a connection between them now.

He took the Studebaker and headed to Mt. Pleasant to bargain for lumber. As he turned off their ranch road to the Mt. Pleasant road, he spotted a down-in-the-heels young cowboy leading a chestnut, which was limping. The cowboy looked up, and Ethan recognized the young man as Woodie Karten. The lanky late teenager with chiseled features didn't appear to be the tough kid Ethan and Odel had awakened one night at his camp where he was following the AT wagons. His bushy hair still hung to his shoulders, which now sagged. He had chapped lips and birdlike eyes. He was walking slowly but stopped when his eyes met Ethan's.

"Following us again?" Ethan asked as he stopped his wagon beside the cowboy.

Woodie removed his hat and took a deep breath.

"No, sir. I went to Arkansas and found my brother's grave. I spent two days there — and decided I didn't want my life to end up like his. I wanted to amount to something — anything — as long as it was worth livin' for. I came lookin' for you. I wanted t' you if I never did another thing."

"How long has it been since you ate?"

The young man shrugged and said, "Maybe 3 days. I won't steal to eat — no matter how bad it gets."

Ethan studied the boy for a couple of moments.

"What are you planning on doing?"

"I don't know. I ain't trained to do nothin'."

Again, Ethan watched the cowboy for any sign of his lying.

"What's the problem with your horse?"

Woodie Karten looked back at his animal.

"He threw a shoe — bruised his hoof."

"Take that road down to where you'll find men cutting trees and a wagon. Ask for Gilmer."

"Gilmer," the kid repeated.

"Tell him who you are, and tell Gilmer Odel can verify it."

"Odel — the one that was with you when you found me?"

"Yes. Tell Gilmer that I gave you a job — but you need a meal."

The cowboy didn't understand.

"A job? Me? After what I did?"

"All you did was follow us. No harm done."

"But I did it for Slade Staker."

"Staker is in jail and will be going to prison. If you want to start over with your life — you can do it here. If you don't work out — for us or for you — you can go on down the road."

Ethan popped his reins, and the wagon moved on. Over his shoulder, Ethan called, "Have them check out your horse, too."

Alby Hinyard delivered a total of six wagons of lumber to the AT with only a down payment. Hinyard was the owner of the sawmill. He and most of Mt. Pleasant had already heard about the recent events in Daingerfield. Hinyard offered to sell whatever lumber Ethan needed on credit because folks were all so pleased to have an outfit like the AT around.

The next few weeks were busy and very productive at the AT.

The homestead plot was cleared except for the stumps, which Gilmer figured to use as part of the building's foundations. Holes were dug, and water pipes were driven into the ground until the crew found clean, clear water. Pumps soon functioned for the cookshack and another trough and pumped to water the horses outside the corral.

The cookshack with two additional rooms for the new cook and her two children was completed a week after the new hire arrived. In a wooden cage of sorts, she brought with her five chickens and one rooster. For one week, she had to cook outdoors using Vella's stove under a tarp. Mrs. Pauley insisted on being called Maude. She and Vella became instant friends. Her son Coy, age 5, and little Della, age 3, loved living first in a tent and then in the new quarters — almost as they loved Brownie and Spot. Gilmer, they saw as a grandfather — and he made them whistles and other toys.

Woodie put together a henhouse. After that, it became Bell's job to collect eggs and feed the chickens. The two children helped her.

Homer told Ethan that Jilson and Isom had worked in the orphanage wood shop and could make tables, chairs, and benches. So they were assigned to that task while all the rest finished the cookshack and dining room. They framed it, laid down planking for the floor, finished the roof, walls, and doors.

The crew worked well together. The brute strength blended with the quickness of teens. Even Woodie blended in. True to his word, he was making something of himself. He was the first one up every day and the last to leave a project for meals or when the light faded.

Once the cookshack and Maud's quarters were done, the new cook and her children moved in. The crew unloaded the wagon that newspaper writer, editor, and publisher Emit Voigtlander had rounded up.

He told her to keep the wagon and her furniture covered until they moved in.

The crew seemed to work with a renewed urgency to finish the dining room portion of the cookshack. From their first meal inside since joining the crew, all the men were thrilled. Mrs. Pauly served blackberry cobbler for dessert on their first night inside. Vella and Bell still helped, but Maude was almost a dust devil in her movements. The cookshack was her domain, and little by little, she had the entire operation under her control.

Bell began spending more time with Coy and Della and the dogs.

The men even worked through light summer rains to erect their bunkhouse. They dug a well between the cookshack and the bunkhouse. Maude insisted everyone wash their hands before coming to eat.

Ethan and Vella seemed to have more and more time to spend together. He learned she was a minister's daughter and married twice before meeting Ethan. She had fallen in love with her first husband, Ned, and ran away from home with him, stealing the money her parents had promised as her dowery. Ned was killed cheating at cards. She humbly returned to her parents, who forgave her. That was when she started teaching school and met her husband, Roman Keifer. Keifer was handsome and made the most of his good looks. She discovered after they were married that he didn't like to work. If he could make it with his looks, he would always try that first. Even though her parents warned her about Keifer, she couldn't or wouldn't see it. But she was young and in love — and afraid of being a widow the rest of her life. Her parents managed to put together a smaller dowery for her second marriage.

"Have you kept in touch with your parents?" Ethan had asked her.

"I wrote them once — right after Roman was killed. Mother wrote back and said neither she nor Daddy wanted to hear from me anymore. They had given up on me."

"When we get the AT up on its feet, maybe you can write them again. Time, I hear, is a great healer."

"Have you written your parents?" she asked him.

"No. I told my brother I was going west — maybe as far as California. I have no idea what they think. I hope my sister is all right — but I don't know." He paused before he said, "My brother, Big John, is honest, hardworking, gentle — but he's a little slow in the head. I know pa was going to leave the horse ranch to me — and I'm not sure Big John can run it by himself. But I can't go back. Even if I wasn't held as guilty by a jury. I'm still a killer of men. Twice counting Flem Staker."

"I don't believe you're a killer or a murderer, Ethan. I don't know what I would have done in your place — in either incident — but I don't see either as murder."

Ethan thought about this for a minute, then cupped Vella's face in his hand and lightly kissed her.

I could write them as Mrs. Andrews and tell them where we are. I'm sure they'd like to know. And nobody would suspect a letter from Texas with our return address.

CHAPTER 32

The plans for the main house had changed as the heat of the summer passed its peak. Instead of the two-room dog run, Vella asked for it to be expanded to three rooms and two open runs. Bell was growing and developing into a young woman, and she would have a space to herself in the middle. Ethan and Vella would occupy the first room together as husband and wife when the buildings were completed. Odel had decided not to share a room with Gilmer but instead chose to take a bed in the bunkhouse with the rest of the men. But the structure had to be finished before any of that would occur.

Brownie and Spot started barking one day as they ran up to an approaching rider. Their tails began swinging as they recognized blacksmith Duff Sprague. He was a broad-shouldered, barrel-chested man with an oval face and wide-set coffee brown eyes. He had big powerful hands but always had a ready smile. The smith was wearing a brass star he had fashioned himself.

"Step down," Ethan said from where he was nailing the roof joists together. "Water your horse and get yourself a drink."

Gilmer had used his water witching skills to locate an ideal spot to drill for water in front of the house while the plank floors were being laid. They had a trough and water pump by the hitching rail where a dipper hung.

By the time Ethan got to the ground, the big blacksmith had loosened his cinch and downed a couple of dippers of the cool water from the pump.

"How are you doing, Duff?" Ethan asked, pumping himself a dipper full.

Rapping on his skull with his knuckles, the town marshal said, "It's harder than anybody expected. But, I'm fine as Kentucky bourbon."

At the mention of Kentucky, Ethan swallowed but made sure nothing showed in his expression. He had flashed back to the night his sister was raped.

"I'm glad they decided to officially make you a lawman," Gilmer called from where he was working on attaching the first shingles. "I hope they're paying you, too."

"Oh, they are — but not much. I'm still only a part-time marshal," the lawman joked.

"Folks don't want law and order until they need it," Ethan said. "You come out to sample the Widow Pauley cooking?"

"I'll be more than happy to do that — but that's not the reason I came."

Ethan motioned to two stumps sawed-off flat. "Pull up a stump and have a seat."

Duff Sprague sat and sighed before he said. "I have some bad news, Ethan."

"Say it. It doesn't get any better with you holding it."

"Slade Staker and two other men broke out of prison in Huntsville."

"I can't say I'm surprised," Ethan said.

"Before he broke out, he said he was going to kill the man who killed his brother."

"Me."

"That's why I rode out to tell you. The telegraph message came through about an hour ago."

Ethan thought a moment, then sighed.

"We've been expecting something like that — eventually. Guess we'll have to set a guard again. We had one for a while until we got the dogs."

Ethan scratched both dogs and petted them, as did the marshal.

"They still remember me," Duff said with a smile.

"I suppose there's no way to guess when to expect them," Ethan said.

"If he follows his pattern, he'll get a gang together and do some robbing before he heads this way. I'll keep my ears open to any more news."

"Thanks. Come on in and have some buttermilk. Those cows we bought are doing well. Lunch will be a while yet. You're not in a hurry, are you?"

"No hurry — and I would like to sample the widow's cookin'. You know it's the talk of the county."

"It deserves to be. Let's get you a glass of buttermilk."

"I also have badges for you and Gilmer," Marshal Sprague said, pulling out two brass stars from his vest. Both were embossed with the word "Deputy."

"Gilmer!" Ethan called. The grizzled man in buckskins lifted his head of flyaway salt and pepper hair from where he worked on the roof. "They've made Duff Sprague town marshal. He wants us to be his deputies. Brought us badges." Ethan held one up for Gilmer to see.

"Mighty pretty," Gilmer said. "Can it wait till lunch?"

"I expect so," Ethan said, pocketing both badges. Then, to the new marshal, he said, "Let's get out of this sun."

❦

The blacksmith/marshal, Duff Sprague, sat at the far end of the long dining table drinking buttermilk. They stayed well out of Maude's and Bell's way as they prepared the upcoming meal. The dogs began to bark out front, and Ethan got up. Before he could get to the door, Gilmer opened it. He was a man who made Ethan think he was a Quaker at first because of the beard he wore with no mustache. The beefy man wore a white shirt with billowing sleeves and dark blue pants tucked into his flat-heeled boots. He also wore a flat cloth hat.

"Captain Bill Cooper," Gilmer said, "meet Ethan Andrews."

Ethan shook the man's hand as the lawman got to his feet and did the same, saying, "Duff Sprague."

"Uncle Bill!" Bell screamed as she ran from the stove to the arms of the sailor.

After a few moments of hugs and cheek kisses, Bell held on to her uncle's arm and introduced Maude, who had stepped down to see what all the fuss was.

"Mrs. Pauly," Captain Cooper said, removing his soft cap.

"Captain," Maude said. "Bell has told us a great deal about you."

"And Bell's letters have informed me about you, Mr. Andrews — and you, Mr. Thebadeau."

"Gilmer and Ethan," Gilmer said. "We ain't very formal around here."

"Duff is Daingerfield Town Marshal. He's also a blacksmith," Ethan finished the introductions.

"I didn't intend to interrupt anything," the captain said.

"Nothing to interrupt," Ethan said. "The marshal just brought us some news and deputy badges." Ethan handed one brass star to Gilmer.

"Bell," Maude said, "go ring the triangle. It's time to call the crew in."

"Yes, ma'am," Bell said and released her uncle's arm and stepped outside. A moment later, the triangle clanged.

"You are more than welcome to join us, Marshal Sprague," Maude said. "You too, Captain."

"I would be honored," Captain Cooper and the marshal said at the same time.

Vella came in the Coy and Della. The children scampered to their seats.

Ethan introduced his wife to Bell's uncle.

"My pleasure, ma'am."

Within a couple of minutes, the men of the crew began streaming in, laughing and talking. They removed their hats and cast curious looks at the lawman and the sea captain. When all the men were there,

Ethan introduced Bell's uncle and Marshal Sprague. The men took their seats and folded their hands for grace.

Ethan said the blessing, asking God to bless them all, and he gave thanks for the meal they were about to eat. Maude went to the stove as all the men stood, grabbed a plate, and lined up by the stove.

CHAPTER 33

Vella helped Maude serve while Bell talked non-stop to her uncle. Finally, when the girl had wound down telling of all their ventures, Ethan was able to speak.

"You've come a long way, Captain."

"Don't let anyone tell you riding on a train is comfortable. I slept better in a force 3 gale."

"We are so glad you put up with it all to come this far."

"Bell is my brother's daughter — my only kin. So I had to see how she was doing?"

"You're Bell's uncle," Maude asked as she served. "I thought she was your sister, Ethan."

"We told everybody that to keep from having to explain awkward things," Ethan said.

"Momma died of the fever, and Papa died trying to fix the wagon when we broke down," Bell explained. "That's when Ethan came along. I had already buried Papa, and he buried Mama. He took me with him to keep anything bad from happening to me."

"Tell everything," Ethan said. Then, to the captain, he said, "She fooled Gilmer and me for a week thinking she was a boy. She called herself Bill Cooper back then."

"But it was better for me to pretend to be Ethan's sister later on," Bell admitted.

"From the things you told me in the letters — which I didn't get for a couple of months, by the way — I was out at sea — you've been a fortunate young lady," he said to his niece.

"More than that, Uncle Bill. I've been loved."

"I can see that," he smiled.

"And she put the money you gave your brother into our partnership — which is becoming the Star AT."

"I saw the sign out by the road," Captain Cooper said."

"We can pay you back as soon as we start making a living here," Ethan said.

"Do you want Bell to come back east with you?" Vella asked.

"I've been thinking about that all the way out here. The problem is, I live in a couple of rented rooms when I'm ashore. So darlin'," he said to Bell, "that's no place for you."

The captain looked around the dining room before he went on.

"If it's agreeable with you," he looked from Ethan to Vella and then to Gilmer, "I'd like to stay around here a few days before we discuss any money. I'm a businessman, and I get the impression this is a growing business."

"You're more than welcome to stay as long as you like," Ethan said.

"It'll be either the bunkhouse with the crew or out in a tent with us," Gilmer said. "As you see, the house isn't finished yet."

"You put up a bunkhouse before your own house?" Captain Cooper asked.

"And a room for the kids and me," Maude cut in as she served seconds to some of the crew across the table.

"Yes, I do want to stay a bit to see how things work around here," the sailor said. "And I don't mind pitching in either."

"Maybe we should hold up on the house and get the sawmill moved while we've got an extra set of hands," Gilmer said.

"Let's finish the roof first and then all hands on the sawmill," Ethan said.

"We'll see to your horse, sir," Woodie Karten said when he was finished.

The following week saw the finishing of the house roof and the construction of the sawmill platform and roof. The crew built skids, and the sawmill machinery was moved. Finally, the entire thing was reassembled at the new site on a rise — one above the level of the 50-year flood plain.

But it took all four mules and all the men to move the heaviest items, the boiler, and the engine. Captain Cooper was of help physically but also with the operation of the steam engine. He said he owned two ocean-going side wheelers and understood the mechanics well.

By the end of the week, the first boards were coming out of the mill. A permanent crew was assigned to the site, with Odel in charge. El was one of the first to volunteer to work on the mill with Odel. The orphanage woodworkers, Jilson, and Isom, were also glad to be part of that workforce.

The rest of the AT turned back to finishing the house.

The schedule of night guards also was set. Two men at a time were set on a nine-hour schedule -- three-hour shifts -- in the woods on both sides of the ranch road. A third man stayed down by the house with the dogs.

Word kept coming in on robberies, and even murders said to be the work of Slade Staker and his new gang. They first hit the land-grant school, the Agricultural and Mechanical College of Texas. A group of 4 stole horses and tack before moving on to Palestine, where they raided a general store and killed the owner's wife. The gang was up to 8 by the time they attacked a freight office in Nacogdoches. Staker and friends killed a deputy sheriff before fleeing. At this point, there were reported to be even dozen members of the gang. Each message told of the gang moving closer and closer to Daingerfield.

At the AT, one of the daily tasks was to check and make sure every pistol, rifle, and shotgun was loaded and in working order.

"It reminds me of expecting pirates," Captain Cooper said one evening checking his own .36 caliber '73 Colt revolver.

Bell asked, "Pirates attacked you?"

"Not attacked — but approached with evil intent. As soon as they got close and my crew rose up along the gunnels with rifles, and we took down half of their crew. Then they suddenly changed course."

"Unfortunately, I don't think the Staker gang will back off no matter what," Ethan said.

CHAPTER 34

A barn raising was held at the AT on the last Saturday of August. The number of wagons and families which showed up amazed Ethan and Vella. Mercantile owner Sanders Hedgecock organized the event. It all started when Maude Pauley, on one of her trips to town for supplies, mentioned that with the sawmill going and the main house was nearly done. So the next project would be to put up a barn.

Everyone knew about Ethan and Gilmer. Town Marshal Duff Sprague introduced the AT to each new arrival. The women brought potluck dishes, cakes, and pies. Maude and Vella set up their cook-shack tables and tarps out on the ground to organize the food. Bell organized the children.

When enough men were there, Duff again stepped forward and directed the building efforts. The AT crew had stacked lumber from their mill for the job according to a list Sanders Hedgecock had set back with Maud. The AT men became parts of the different crews at the Marshal's direction, and all went to work.

It was amazing to watch the effort come together. Like ants, the men and older boys swarmed the sight beyond the corral and knocked together the frames of all four sides.

The man rotated from time to time to the picnic-style meal where food, water, and even tea and beer were waiting for them.

When the frames were ready, ropes with block-and-tackle were attached, and coordinated groups pulled the skeleton form flat on the ground up into the air, were daring men at the very top secured one section to another. Support posts were erected inside for stalls and the hayloft. Planks were hoisted, and the roof grew until it was done on both sides and the structure was solid.

The team working on the barn doors moved them into place where they were hinged. This included the loft doors and braced hoisting arm above the loft doors. Other men nailed boards in place to cover the sides, and additional thinner strips of lumber were secured over each slit where one plank met the next.

While all this was going on, some of the women pitched in and helped Vella plant a fall garden.

By late afternoon, the barn was standing and ready for use. Ethan was given the honor of driving the very last nail. As soon as he stepped back from striking the final blow, a roar went up from everyone.

All enjoyed dinner on the ground, and when a fiddle and banjo were produced, the dancing began. It was almost midnight under another bright moon before the new friends and neighbors had packed up and left the AT.

As the last wagon pulled out, Ethan had his arm around Vella's waist and a satisfied look on both their faces.

"Now, if we only had a place of our own to go to — and shut the door," Vella said.

<hr />

The next day was a day for baths and church. Ethan drove the Studabaker, loaded with Bell, the would-be-robbers, and Woodie Karten. The McMullins all went fishing along with Gilmer and Odel.

Monday was the day for finishing the main house. Walls, windows, and doors were all completed for all three separate rooms under the main house roof. Each room had a potbelly stove. There was also one for Maude's rooms, the cookshack, and the bunkhouse. In rooms of the main house, double beds were erected. A mail-ordered mattress pad of corn husks or horsehair was laid in each. This was the same kind of mattress Ethan had ordered for Maude and her children, as well as for the bunkhouse.

That night before he closed the door to their room, Ethan asked Vella if she was sure this was what she wanted. She understood the question and was gratified by his thoughtfulness. She answered him with a long, passionate kiss.

At breakfast the following day, Maude said to Vella, "You didn't get much of a honeymoon."

"I couldn't have asked for anything more," Vella answered with a smile.

CHAPTER 35

Ethan, Gilmer, with the input from Captain Cooper, decided that the outlaws would never attempt to approach the AT through the woods and meadows behind the homeplace. The thinking was that the outlaws were lazy and would come via the easiest route.

The night watch scheduled included Ethan, Gilmer, and everyman in the AT. Captain Cooper even participated. They held their positions until relieved.

The danger signal was to be a single shot from both lookouts. In front of the main house, the man kept time and ensured that the guards were changed every three hours.

The night of the Commanche Moon, a single rider approached the ranch road and paused at the entrance. He peered into the woods and down the road. After his survey, he eased his horse around and headed back towards Daingerfield. Several minutes later, a baker's dozen riders slowly came up the main road. At their leader's signal, they all headed down the ranch road to the main house at a full gallop.

Ship McMulliens fired the first shot into the air as the gang passed his position in the woods on the north side. His shot was followed by a second one from Woodie Karten on the right. Both headed for the main house, staying in the trees as they hurried. Isom Ganninger, posted with the dogs, fired a warning shot into the air with his shotgun. Spot and Brownie leaped to their feet and began barking,

Ethan sprang from the arms of Vella in bed to grab his pants, pull on his boots, and strap on his gun belt. He lifted his Winchester off its pegs over the fireplace and yanked open the door.

The outlaws continued to race forward up the road, shooting into the air and yelling savage noises.

Brownie and Spot headed toward the approaching hoard, yapping, and barking.

Captain Cooper met Ethan on the porch. He was armed with a pistol. Both men heard the sound of Gilmer's boots retreating at a run back in the corral's direction.

When the gang reached the open front yard, they pulled up, aiming their weapons at Ethan and the captain.

"Where is Ethan Andrews?" their leader shouted.

This was the first time Ethan had seen Slade Staker since the incident at the Broken Wheel saloon back in Arkadelphia. Ethan only remembered that Slade was taller than his brother Flem. He'd paid little attention to the pair until Gilmer had entered, saying he had found their missing mules. Both brothers had turned and began firing at Gilmer. Ethan had leaped up and shot the shorter brother under the arm, killing him when the bullet tore through the man's heart. The gun smoke in the room had hidden Gilmer and the older Slaker brother, who rushed out, still shooting at where Gilmer had entered.

This time the man was sitting on a black Arabian. His features were chiseled and rangy, with a twisted snarl.

"What do you want with him?" Captain Cooper asked as Isom backed up and loaded a fresh shell in his double-barreled shotgun.

"He killed my brother — I'm going to kill him!" Slade said. "Then we're going to burn this place to the ground."

"You think there are enough of you to do that?" Ethan asked.

"There are 14 of us. I count three of you. Who's going to stop us."

"I will!" came the voice of Woodie Karten in the woods behind them.

The outlaws looked but couldn't locate the voice or the man.

"OK, four of you."

The loft door or the barn was kicked open, and Gilmer aimed with his Sharps. "You're going to be the first to die!"

"There are more of us," came the voice of Rollo McMulliens from the edge of the rise beside the gang. The levering of rounds into Winchesters was heard from beside him.

"Believe it!" Odel called from the other side of the main house where he stood aiming his Sharps

"You are surrounded," Ethan said. "Start shooting, and all of you will die."

"Oh, yeah?" Slade Staker said, aiming at Ethan and firing.

Suddenly, the air was full of bees and hornets darting from the blasts of gunfire coming from the outlaw gang and from all the AT crew around it. Flashes and smoke stabbed out of the outlaws and from the woods and berms on both sides, plus the main house.

Slade's shot missed its target, but Ethan's did not. Slade was pitched back off his mount from an additional shot by Gilmer. The other outlaws shot in every direction. Odel took out another outlaw with his first shot from beside the house. After that, the AT crew cut down others. Bell stepped out from the door of her room, carefully aiming and firing her pistol. Captain Cooper got off a couple of shots from his Colt revolver before being hit and thrown back. But he kept firing. Bell hurried over to her uncle, her smoking Smith and Wesson in her hand.

The gunfight continued with shots from the rest of the AT crew coming in from the woods near Odel. All the outlaws were cleared from their saddles — including the three who tried to abandon the fight and get away. The battle lasted less than half a minute. The outlaws had ridden into a crossfire and suffered the consequences.

Finally, there were no more shots from either side. Instead, a thick haze of smoke hung all around. The horses wandered around frantically but aimlessly. Two animals stumbled from bullets they had taken.

When it was quiet, Ethan stepped over to the captain. "Where are you hit?"

"The arm. I'll be all right. Check on everyone else."

Isom was down with a shot in the leg. Ethan pulled the young man's belt out of his jeans and tightened it around his leg above the wound. Vella was there an instant later.

"I'll look after Isom," she said.

Ethan left her to tend to the youngster and stood.

"Hold your fire!" Ethan shouted to his men. He walked into the milling horses and found dead and wounded outlaws. He picked up pistols and rifles, flinging them away from the site.

The rest of the AT crew came forward, ready for more shooting.

Homer shot one horse on its side, kicking and squirming in pain. The animal had absorbed three shots, and there was no way it could recover. Ship McMulliens began gathering the loose horses.

There were only two of the outlaws who were wounded but still alive. Ethan pulled one of them to his feet. Woodie Karten did the same for another.

CHAPTER 36

One of the wounded outlaws had been hit twice. One shot in the right arm and the other through his stomach and liver. There wasn't much Doc Manheim could do for him. They gave him water, and he died where he had fallen.

The other had a chunk taken out of his hipbone. The physician stopped the bleeding and wrapped his wound. In turn, he was able to identify the other members of the gang laid out in the dirt. A couple only had one name that he knew of, but he told Marshal Sprague what he knew.

Doc Manheim had Isom, and Captain Cooper and the wounded outlaw moved to the cookshack. Bell went with them, with Maude leading the way.

Bill Cooper bit his lip but never complained as Doc sewed up the tear in his arm. The sea had made him a tough man.

They had to hold young Isom Ganninger.

"I'm sorry, son," the physician told the boy, "but it's going to get worse before it gets any better. I have to dig that slug out of you, or you will die of lead poisoning." Isom was given a belt to bite on as the doctor located and extracted the .44 slug from his thigh.

By the time Doc Manheim finished stitching Isom up, the boy had passed out. Doc Manheim told Ethan and Gilmer, "This boy will need a crutch, and he will have to keep the weight off the leg for at least a week. Even after that, he will have to take it easy. It will be about a month or more before he's fully functional."

"Jilson can carve him a crutch," Gilmer said.

"We'll keep an eye on him," Vella said. "Tomorrow, we'll get him one of the benches he made to sit on outside. I'm sure we can find things for him to do until he can move around."

"I'll see to that," Gilmer said.

"Duff," Ethan ask the marshal, "what do we do with the horses?"

"They're yours, I figure."

"But there are a couple of very nice horses here. Including the Arabian Slade Staker was riding."

"And all the brands have been altered with running irons. I don't know how I'd ever find out who owned 'em. If I do, I'll let you know."

※

Marshal Sprague used Gilmer's wagon to haul off the dead to an unclaimed field where the first Daingerfield had burned down. This became the area's boot hill.

The AT didn't see the Marshal for 2 days until he was back with a telegraphed message authorizing the Atlas Bank to pay the sum of 5 thousand 200 dollars for the bounties of the identified outlaws.

Ethan looked down at the telegram a moment before he said, "I sure don't like making money this way."

"Texas figures you earned it," Marshal Sprague said.

"It's the first time I've collected bounty money." He looked over at Vella standing beside him. She smiled and nodded. "They earned their bounties. We'll make good use of the funds.

Ethan turned back to Duff Sprague, saying, "Thank you."

"Don't begrudge yourself, Ethan. Like it or not, what the AT did the other night was a service."

Sprague tipped his hat and returned to Daingerfield.

"I guess you'll not be needing any of my money," Captain Bill

Cooper said, taking a drag on his pipe and leaning against the hitching rail beside Bell.

"Your money?" Ethan asked.

"I was seriously thinking about an offer to buy into this outfit — to the tune of 2 thousand dollars."

"For what?"

"A partnership — a silent partnership. I'm going back to Norfork — and maybe back to sea. But I'm more than the ship's captain. Like I told you before, I'm a businessman. I own three ships — and I know a good business when I see one. The AT is one."

"We've not turned a profit yet," Ethan said.

"No, but you will. Between the sawmill, the horses you're going to raise, and the crops — whatever they are — cotton, I expect…"

"No," Ethan looked back and Vella. "Everybody around here is raising cotton. We thought we'd do something different — some fruits — apples, figs …"

"Blackberries and Raspberries," Vella finished the thought.

"And Gilmer still wants to run a couple dozen cattle."

"See what I'm thinking? You're looking ahead. This is going to be a profitable place. But I had a couple of other motives."

"Like what?" Bell asked.

"Someday, I'm going to retire. No time soon, mind you — but someday. And when I do, I've decided I want to get to somewhere far away from the ocean. This seems like a good spot."

"You'll always be welcome here, Bill," Ethan said with agreements from both Vella and Bell.

"Yeah, but I'd like a nice big room — and a couple of comfortable rocking chairs."

"Why a couple?" Ethan asked.

"One for me and one for my wife."

"You're going to get married," Bell said, jumping up and down in place.

"Yes — and that's the other reason I wanted to buy in the AT. I'm going to be shanghaiing part of your crew?"

"How do you plan to do that?" asked Ethan.

"I plan to marry one and adopt the other two," the captain said with a straight face.

"Maude, Coy, and Della," Vella said with a slight smile.

"I've been that obvious?" Bill laughed.

"Those were sparks I thought I saw between you two," Vella said.

"That's wonderful, Uncle Bill," Bell said. "I'll have cousins."

"We won't leave until you have yourself a new cook — but if a silent partnership is available, I — we — Maude and me — would like to buy in."

"Done," Ethan said.

THE END

TWO FREE E-BOOKS

[Murder in Muleshoe]
If you were murdered would they try to find the killer or plan him a parade?

[Guns Along The Rio]
In 1858, two fresh-off-the-ranch 17-year-olds join the Texas Rangers. What could possibly go wrong?

GO TO: http://eepurl.com/dKEi_Y

ABOUT THE AUTHOR

Jack R. Stanley is an award-winning novelist, playwright, and screenwriter. As an officer and combat photographer in Vietnam, he earned the Bronze. He earned both his M.A. and his Ph.D. at the University of Michigan in Ann Arbor in Radio-TV-Film. His doctoral dissertation was on the TV series GUNSMOKE. Still married to his gifted high school sweetheart, Stanley was TV Area Head at The University of Texas at Austin's Department of Radio-TV-Film. He later moved to deep-south Texas and the Lower Rio Grande Valley for a challenging position with The University of Texas-Pan American. Here he taught Theatre-TV-Film for 30 years in the Department of Communication serving as Department Chair at U.T.P.A. for 11 years. He now lives in the Texas Panhandle where he writes his fiction. His webpage is www.jackrstanley.com.

ALSO BY JACK R, STANLEY

ALSO BY THE AUTHOR

Novels

[Westerns]

Guns Along The Rio

West Of The Frio

A Hard Line Between The Rios

The Mormon Marshal

Along The Outlaw Trail

The Gavel and the Gun

13 Steps To Hell

Massacre At Going Snake

Incident At Lajitats

Pancho's Pilot

Return to Redemption

Occurrence At Latigo

The Hussy and the Hardcase

Some Men Need Killin'

Ode To An Outlaw

[Science Fiction]

A New War

[Political Fiction]

The Reluctant President

The Reluctant Incumbent

The Reluctant Candidate

The Elected President

{Vietnam}

Through A Lens Darkly: Vietnam

{Mysteries}

Murder In Muleshoe

Corpse In Canyon

The Lovecraft Murders

Short Stories

Tales From The Alaskan Gold Rush

Klondike Justice

Dangerous Camp On The Kenai

The Winds of Skagway

Screenplays

6 and 10

The 7th Luger

Afternoon Delight

Angel's Revenge

Between Love And Murder

Blood Drive

Death Scene

The Defection of Grigori Dorsky

The Evil Eye

Fatty and Hearst

Gideon: The Horse That Saved Texas

Hell In Paradise

Hollowpoint

Holiday For An Assassin

Horse Thief Hollow

Incident A tLajitas

Love, Lust, & Life

Mom & Apple Pye

Pancho's Pilot

The Prometheus Peril

The Rape of Sarah Quinn

Reservations

River of Tears

Seven Reasons Why

The Thing About Love

The Texas Rattlesnake Murders

Too Good To Be True

The Vampire Rose

A Violent End

The Virgin Casanova

Plays

Antigone In Texas

Cyrano

The Last Virgin From Las Vegas

The Seven Keys

The Unwed Widow

Made in the USA
Middletown, DE
20 February 2022